THE yleros CONTRACT

BY JIM MARCUS

The Yleros Contract

by Jim Marcus

November, 2025

This book is set in Lato Regular 9/13
Titles in Lato Heavy 16/20

ISBN: 979-8-9936679-0-4

WARNING

There are extreme sex acts depicted in this book that shouldn't be attempted casually by anyone. Please be consensual and responsible in considering emulating anything from this book.

That Madness is a part of Love,

and Love comes before Law

Chapter 1

The thing that was immediately jarring was the familiarity of it all.

Jonah noticed that the club was directly behind the mall. When he was much younger, he'd gotten his ears pierced for the very first time at this mall. And, although he didn't live in this neighborhood, he could see the entirety of it on the back of his eyelids when he closed his eyes.

It was as close to being "his mall" as any place would be.

Eve put her hand on his leg as they pulled the car into the parking lot. "Are you sure about this?"

He looked over at her. Her long hair looked pitch black in the dim light tonight. He knew that light would make it explode in deep purpose and red tones, subtle, mysterious. But that light wasn't here.

Here was dark.

Jonah nodded. He felt her squeeze his leg as hard as she could. This was her way of asserting authority in their relationship. Or, it had been over the last few months, as they explored switching. She knew he liked firm touches. She knew he liked to feel like she could physically stand up to him when she was in charge.

And she did.

Eve pulled him in and forced her tongue into his mouth, pushing it past his lips as though she could dig back into his head. He felt his arms drop to his sides in acceptance.

When he was in charge, Eve would make her arms smooth, soft, yielding, offering no resistance. He tried to emulate that, fighting against his native instinct to fight back.

She moved her hand up to his throat and pressed down on it as she kissed. The kiss was long and wet and Jonah tried to let himself feel his own victimhood in it.

He tried to feel helpless but wanting.

She leaned over his body and opened the door, pushing him out. She put down the parking brake and stepped out on her side. To Jonah, it felt like her nearness to the club was empowering her, making her bold.

He didn't hate it.

They stepped up to the front of the club without talking. There was a lit symbol on the front that looked like a lower case "y" in a circle. Eve opened the door and pulled him in. As they approached an inner door in a small foyer, she pulled out the key, positioning it at the door lock for the first time.

This was the key she had been sent when applying. Jonah had filled out all the paperwork, answered every question, until, finally, a month later, the key had arrived. It was all metal, black, with the same symbol as he had seen on the front of the club.

They moved into a larger interior area. There was a tall, blonde, stern-looking woman behind a table. She wore a dark suit with a black shirt beneath it, open at the neck. She motioned to him. Jonah tried to remember everything he'd been told. He pulled his shoes off and placed them on the table. The woman ignored him and spoke to Eve.

She smiled. "You must be Eve. It's great to meet you." The woman reached over and shook Eve's hand. Her face lit up.

Eve took her hand. "Are you Grey? You look exactly like I thought you would."

Grey's voice was light and belied her stern appearance. "I am. And you are so much prettier than your picture."

She leaned over the table and kissed her. Jonah was surprised at the intimacy of it as he removed his pants and folded them on the table. He was wearing a black jock strap that left his ass visible. He pulled his shirt off, revealing a black t-shirt. He pushed the clothing back and pulled on the black kneepads waiting for him on the table.

Eve and Grey were laughing as the blonde woman pulled out the small graphite piece of equipment and pointed to the table.

Jonah looked at Eve. Eve looked frustrated for a moment. "Sweetheart, put your wrist on the table, palm up."

Jonah whispered to her, "What's happening?"

Eve pulled him back, grabbing him between the legs. "Jo. You get a little dot tattoo every time you're here. Do you understand?"

He nodded. This was something no one had told him about. This would be his very first tattoo. Even if it was only a dot. He placed his hand on the table.

Grey grabbed his hand roughly, flattening it on the table. She pointed to her side where Jonah saw the ten rules as she slowly dug the tattoo gun into his wrist and made a tiny circle, filling it in. It was dark in the foyer, with only a green glow from under the tables to fill the room. As Jonah's eyes adjusted to the darkness, even more pervasive than outside, his eyes scanned the rules:

1. *Men will dress appropriately. Men will never have their ass covered.*

2. *Men will not speak unless asked by a woman directly.*

3. *Men will serve the women*

4. *Men will orally service a woman if she pushes his head down*

5. *Men will not stop until they are pushed away*

6. *Men will accept that women may need to piss on and in them*

7. *Men will accept that women may need to hit them*

8. *Men will bend over and accept penetration from a woman if needed*

9. *If a man is not with an owner, he may be taken upstairs*

10. *Men will not discuss or complain amongst themselves*

The dot hurt but he was afraid to touch it. There was a drop or two of blood on it. He shook his wrist as Eve kissed Grey again, a longer kiss this time, and pulled him through the door.

The lighting here was brighter, but still dim. It looked like an art gallery in places, with white walls covered in art. There were candles everywhere, flickering. At one point, Jonah couldn't see a single light source that wasn't a candle. Eve pulled him into an enclosed area and whispered,

"What do you think so far?"

Jonah felt her hands on his waist, pulling at him and he could tell he was getting turned on by the environment. He whispered back, "Is it okay if I talk here?"

She nodded and kissed him, again, pushing at him, forcing her tongue into his mouth. She held the back of his head and he went limp, letting her do what she wanted.

"You can answer me. If I ask you a question. Ok, do you understand?"

He nodded, "Yes, sir. I can answer if you ask me a question."

She turned and pushed him face forward into the wall. His head hit the surface and he put his hands up against it. She slapped him in the back of the head and then punched him in the back. Still whispering, she responded, "But only if I ask, ok?"

Jonah felt the pain spread throughout his body. "Yes, sir."

She pressed his head against the wall with one hand and with the other began punching his ass. At first, she focused on his ass cheeks, one at a time, and then, finally, focused her energies in the center, right on his asshole. She hit him harder and harder in the asshole as Jonah spread his legs for her.

Eve laughed at his legs spreading. "Good boy."

Jonah was breathing heavily. "Yes, Sir."

Eve seemed to lose it, becoming angry. She yelled out, "I didn't ask a question, Jonah."

She pounded at him, digging her knuckles in as two other women stepped into the space. They looked at Eve, "Are you ok?"

Eve punched twice more before turning to them. "Yes, I just need to make him understand shit. You know what I mean?"

They laughed. Jonah couldn't see them. The one with the higher voice said, "You should make him spread his ass with his hands so you can get up in there."

The other woman laughed, "Yes."

Eve laughed along, "Yes, Jo, use your hands."

He pressed his face against the wall and reached around, pulling his ass apart. Eve punched at his open asshole. Jonah winced but tried to stay steady. He tried to imagine what the other two women were doing. He'd never done anything like this in front of people. Suddenly, he lost his erection.

But it still felt exciting?

Jonah bent down lower on the wall, sticking his ass in the air. He could feel himself sliding down the wall as one of the women asked, "Do you want a bat or a strop or whip or something?"

Eve was breathing hard. "Damn, yes. Do you have a strop?"

"One sec." There was a rush as the woman went to get it. Jonay slid down the wall and onto his knees, his ass in the air, hands still pressed to his asscheeks keeping it open.

"What the fuck. Did I tell you to drop?" Eve kicked him. The kick hit right where she had been punching him, on his open asshole. It hurt. The second one grazed his balls, in the jock strap. He let out a gasp and she kicked him twice harder. "Shut up."

Jonah hadn't moved his hands. His ass was spread as wide as possible. The other woman must have gotten back with the strop because the next thing he felt was the lithe leather belt-like implement come down on his rectum. Eve had never hit him this hard or this way when they were alone.

Although he had hit HER with a belt.

He closed his eyes. A reddish black wave ran across his corneas behind his pursed lids every time she connected. The other woman said, "He's not counting."

Eve growled at him. "Count!"

He started counting as the leather tool came down over and over on his exposed ass. The pain was impossibly intense, So much so that when she missed and hit his hands, it was like a vacation, a blessed relief from the next assault. He counted to fifty as the three women talked and laughed. Halfway through, he couldn't understand the words they used.

The last four hits were performatively hard. He could tell Eve was winding up to attack and bring it down as hard as she could. Jonah's head dipped below his shoulders and hit the ground. His face was filled with tears. He could feel his shoulders move up and down with his heavy breaths.

One of the women seemed to step closer. The pain was overwhelming as his ass was violated. He could feel her fingers inside him. She sounded amazed, "This hole is so hot now. It's like a thousand degrees." She pushed her fingers in and out and laughed.

Eve Knelt down hard between his legs.

He could feel her hand exploring inside him. She was speaking to the women when she said, "I bet it doesn't even hurt anymore. But this will feel good."

Jonah felt nothing for a moment then the ice cold of some kind of lubricant as she poured it and massaged it between his legs. He kept his hands in place and took in a sharp breath.

The other woman said, mockingly, "ooh, check this out. I'm sorry, Mr. asshole. Do you still love me? Yes I do. Look at that. He felt an object dig into his open ass while the women laughed. "See, no hard feelings, mr. Strop."

Eve sounded amazed, "Oh my god, I wouldn't let something that just beat me like that fuck me."

The woman with the higher voice was getting excited. "Oh, mr. strop, let me take you inside me all the way."

He felt one of them step on his head as the object slid deeply inside him, into places he couldn't feel anymore. He felt it in his abdomen and he could tell that the leather part was barely poking out of his asshole.

The other woman called out, "Don't lose it up there."

Eve's voice sounded comforting, even though what she said wasn't. "It's ok. I can get it back anytime. He felt the warm spray of liquid on his ass while the strop was still in. Someone in boots kicked him until he rolled over onto his back. He looked up at Eve and saw her pissing on him, her arm wrapped around one of the other women. She was a dark woman with deep red hair and was pissing on him as well. He tried to shield his eyes from the one light behind them but felt a foot kick his hand away as another woman knelt on his face and began to slowly pee in his mouth. He opened up and swallowed the briny liquid in waves, his hands at his sides, while she pulled at his hair.

Eve pulled the car around later that night and made him lie in the back seat on a blanket. They left his clothes behind.

At home, she reached in and pulled the strop out of his ass before allowing him to bathe in the dark with a single candle. He cried in the tub.

When he came to bed, he had masturbated already in the tub, but he still came in her as she rode him.

***

It had been 2 weeks since they had gone to the Yleros club and Jonah could see a difference in Eve. She seemed to laugh louder. Her smile when she looked at him was bigger. She even ordered dessert at dinner, something she rarely did.

She had responded to that night in an unexpected way. She seemed bigger now, more alive. As they sat on the couch watching a movie, she paused it to tell him a joke. That was something. Jonah thought, "Had Eve ever told him a joke? I mean, she was situationally very funny, quick, light hearted.

But a full joke?

A few nights later he caught her kissing the little dot on his wrist. He laughed, "You like my tattoo?"

She smiled at him in her pajama shirt. "Honestly, I fucking love it."

And there it was again. Her face lit up. Jonah was still processing how he felt. He was still potentially on the fence about the experience but he was not on the fence in any way about the effect on her.

She was electric. Eve was never a quiet or restrained person. She screamed at shows when they saw her favorite bands. She yelled on the dance floor. She even moaned as loudly as possible when, on their third date, he had taken her in an ally, right beside the garage for a house cleaning service, yanking her pants down to her ankles and fucking her for the first time. She liked that story.

She liked the idea they almost got caught.

But this was different. This was grander, more explosive.

Jonah felt himself whisper as he said "When do I get the next one?"

Eve's face burst into a smile. She pulled up her pajama top to expose her white cotton panties. She reached between her legs. He could see her pushing her panties inside her pussy with her fingers, rubbing it, wiping her cunt on them. Then, in one swift movement she slid them off and kneeled up, grabbing Jonah by the throat and shoving her soiled panties into his mouth.

He opened wide and nearly choked on them while she pushed them down deep with her fingers. She slapped his face over and over, pushing him down onto the bed. She pulled his hair and climbed up onto his face.

Jonah inhaled, tasting her in his mouth and smelling her as she mounted his face. She smelled amazing. She held onto his hair tightly as she seemed to be trying hard to muster something. He could see her pussy twitch. The tiny hole opened and closed and she started to drip into his mouth. He closed his eyes and felt the drizzle of her piss soaking her panties in his open mouth. He tried to drink it without choking, filtering it through the beautiful soiled rag in his mouth. It dripped into his hair and down his face and he could feel her slapping him.

"Don't make a mess. Stop it. Suck." He knew it was impossible for him to get it all, but he tried, harder and harder. She slapped him again and let go, with one last gush. His cock was hard now as he tried to drink the salty liquid through the cotton wad in his mouth. She slid down over his belly and impaled herself on his dick, slapping him in the face again.

"Don't make a fucking mess. Jesus."

He tried to apologize but she didn't care. She slid up and down on his dick. He bucked and came but she kept going. He tried his best to work past the refraction and stay hard, waiting for her orgasm two minutes later. She came while slapping his face.

She rolled off of him, laughing. Ripping open his mouth and pulling the wad of wet cotton out. She spread her legs against the dresser and wiped her cunt with the dirty panties. Jonah had never seen her behave so raw. It was just different.

And he liked the abandon. The disregard for convention. He felt close to her.

She threw the panties at him and climbed into bed. "Put these in the wash and come back and suck my clit like a dick."

He stepped into the bathroom to throw them in the wash. Even without the lights, he could see his face was red. He looked like an animal.

He felt like it, too.

He went back to the bedroom to see Eve with her legs spread. He rolled over onto the bed and put his face between her legs. Ordinarily, he would go down on her for 20 minutes or so and she would cum, passively. Tonight she grabbed his head and moved it multiple times, pressing it where it needed to be. She came into his mouth three times before she pushed him away.

Before he fell asleep, she called out in the dark. "I say Saturday night. One more tattoo."

He fell asleep dreaming about the little tattoo. He woke up at 3am. He'd seen that tattoo before.

Where had he seen it?

Chapter 2

Jonah got his second tattoo on Saturday.

The woman named Grey was there again, dressed nearly identically. This time, though, her shirt was a deep maroon. He looked at her face as she tattooed him for just a second before she slapped him and pointed down.

He directed his eyes downward. It was clear she had no intention of speaking to a man there. Eve shook her head and smirked. She took a number that matched the number attached to Jonah's clothes. It was his understanding, based on their conversation on the way there, that if he behaved, he'd get them back.

Eve stepped into the club with purpose tonight. Jonah had woken up and heard her on the phone a few nights ago, discussing what it had to offer. She grabbed him by the arm and dragged him with her as she stepped through a door he hadn't seen before into a large, wide open space. The lights were blues and greens and all seemed to be coming from giant monitors in front of reclining seats and the water below. Each of the reclining seats dipped, at their bottoms, into a blue, shimmering pool.

Eve stood near one of the chairs. Jonah looked over and saw a few occupied and realized what was expected of him. He slid into the indentation that left a hole in the center of the chair seat. his legs were wrapped around an open column in front of the chair, in the water, as he placed his head, face up, in the center indent of the chair.

He slipped his hands into the grooves on either side of the chair and felt the straps tighten, binding them in.

He could see Eve removing her skirt and climbing on the chair. She shifted until her naked asshole was right on his mouth. He opened and stuck his tongue out, docking her into place with it.

She pushed down, letting his tongue slide deeper into her open ass. Jonah couldn't move his arms or his legs. He felt the water below him on his bare ass, soaking his jock strap. For a moment he felt vulnerable, realizing anyone could just step on or hit his cock and he'd be unable to do anything about it.

Against his will, that thought unexpectedly made him erect.

He'd seen them when he'd walked in the room. The nude men walking through the water, attending to the women's feet. Jonah couldn't see anything right now, though, except the curve of Eve's ass over his face.

He slowly licked at her asshole, feeling it open for him. Eve laughed a bit as the water splashed while one of the men moved toward her. Jonah felt the man's knee bump up against his balls while the man worked to give her a pedicure.

Eve rubbed her asshole in his face, intentionally, breathing a little heavier as he dug it deeper into her. Jonah felt her intensity increase as a little hum began to grow. Eve may have been using a vibrator, or the man was pleasuring her with one. He licked harder as she pushed, moving back and forth.

The tvs in the room were playing a movie that Jonah couldn't make out. He couldn't hear anything now but the sound of the vibrator tool. The juices from Eve's pussy were dripping back between her asscheeks, into his mouth and he scrambled to swallow them all. He felt her squirt lightly in his mouth and then cum with large, bucking movements.

For a moment, he nearly panicked, unable to breathe. Until she lifted her ass a bit. The low light filled in the space, making Jonah wish he could shield his eyes.

Eve leaned forward and her wet cunt slipped over his face.

Jonah sucked even harder, Working on her clit and the upper area of her vulva, he let himself inhale her, getting lost in the perfect smell of her pussy. She lifted herself a bit and put her hand behind her to steady herself. Jonah could tell by the slightness of her movements that she was probably having one of the men still work on her toes. She leaned forward and began to piss.

It didn't come out slowly this time. It was a barrage, slamming into him, forcing its way down his throat, pouring onto the seat and into the pool. Jonah heard Eve laugh, along with the man, as she experienced the power of her own piss. Jonah did his best but began to choke as the stream slowed. The man in front of her laughed and she heard Eve slap him.

Had he spoken out of turn?

She sat back down hard on his face and the entire chair leaned back, reclining as if on command. Jonah tried to track what was happening, but it was hard when you couldn't see anything. The chair was nearly flat now, the back having lowered as Eve laid back. She lifted her ass in the air and for a moment, Jonah could see the man climbing onto the chair, his naked cock aiming at her cunt. Jonah saw the head disappear into the pussy in his face just as Eve sat down hard on him.

She let out a long moan. Her ass spread wider as she wrapped her legs around the man, who was slowly pumping into her.

"Slowly. Slowly. Fucking slow down."

Jonah heard the man say "Yes Sir." meekly as he slowed.

Eve slapped him repeatedly. She whispered loudly, "Did I ask a question?"

Jonah felt the man's dick moving in and out of her. He pressed his tongue upward, into her ass again, and he could feel it through the slight membrane separating her cervix from her anus. She'd never fucked another man in front of him before, certainly not on top of him. He felt exposed and lost, with no idea what to do next except to keep sucking.

This was all new territory.

"Shut the fuck up and fuck me. Oh, like that. I love that stupid fucking dick."

Jonah sucked at her as he listened to her direct the scene he couldn't see. He imagined he could describe the man's cock just by the shape he felt on his tongue from inside her ass. She began bucking and undulating, pressing against him, slamming into his nose. He nearly bit his tongue as he felt her climax, a stream of her pussy juice washing onto his face from below her.

The man kept fucking, faster and faster. Eve's voice was a whisper, "Tell me when you cum.Then shut up."

"Yes, sir. I'm cumming. I'm cumming." He slammed into her, compressing Jonah's face, forcing his head into the cushion beneath him. Jonah panicked, sucking and licking as the man came hard into her with one last thrust. He felt them both breathing hard for a moment.

Eve seemed to be kissing the man before she said, matter of factly, "Get up. Finish my toes."

Jonah felt his member pull out of Eve's box with his tongue dug into her rectum. The back of the seat began to rise and she sat up.

She reached out behind her and grabbed jonah's short shock of brownish hair, using his face like a towel to wipe off her pussy. Jonah's face slipped into her cunt, to be met with the strong bite of a man's semen. Eve opened and closed her hole over his face, almost like she was just casually doing kegels. Cum poured into his open mouth, filling it with a salty, base thickness. He extended his throat to swallow it as more came out.

Eve was holding his head beneath her so he couldn't move. For a second , Jonah panicked, unable to do anything but swallow over and over. He licked and cleaned her pussy, doing his best to suck out all the sticky, milky liquid until, finally, she stood up. He saw the perfect curve of her ass as she stepped over his feet. For a moment, he thought she might help him up but then he realized that would not happen. He lifted himself up and realized how long he had been there, trapped as part of the chair. He felt a bit woozy.

Eve slapped him on the ass and then pointed. "Go, over there and get cleaned up. Then, meet me in the room behind the showers.

Jonah tried to maintain his balance as he made his way to the showers. There was a white, well lit room with about 20 shower stalls. Each of them had a giant number displayed in black tile. As he stepped in, a naked man reached for his clothes. He pulled off his drenched shirt and black jock strap, the only two articles of clothing he owned, and stepped over to open stall 7 The water turned on immediately and it was comfortingly warm. The lights above were warm as well.

It looked to him like about half the stalls were full of other men washing up. In front were what looked like a row of mirrors. Clearly, though, they were two way mirrors. Jonah made a point to clean up as fast as he could and meet up with Eve.

Suddenly, over the speaker system, he heard a woman's voice. "Number 7, jack your cock."

He looked around. The man in the 8th's shower stall nodded to him and pointed.

Jonah took his semi-flaccid dick into his right hand and began to pump it. He moved his hand up and down, pointing himself at the mirrors. He felt the water run down his back and it felt amazing. For a moment, he tried to pretend he was alone.

"Number 7, jack harder."

He started to pull at his shaft harder, pumping it like he would if he just wanted to get off before bed. Making it hard. He still wasn't quite all the way hard.

"Number 8, help him with your mouth."

The man in the stall next to him was a slightly smaller latin man. He dropped to his knees and crawled over, placing his hands on Jonah's ass and licking at his balls. Jonah's prick rose imperiously as the man licked, making it easier for Jonah to pump harder.

The voice called out again, this time laughing. It seemed like a different woman. "Number 8, now eat that ass. Eat it."

The wiry man quickly crawled around Jonah's body and buried his face between the globes of his ass. His tongue darted in and out of Jonah's ass. Jonah gasped involuntarily for a second while the man explored his asshole with his tongue. He pointed his cock directly at the mirror in front of him and jerked it hard while the other man's mouth slurped away, sucking his open ass.

"Facefuck his asshole, number 8. Harder."

Jonah grabbed on to the wall of the stall separating the two areas as the man pushed his tongue again and again into his ass. He looked down and he could see the precum at the tip of his dick. He let out a small moan and pumped until his cum shot out onto the ground, lost in the shower spray.

As the speaker came back on, he heard the celebrations of the women. A new one said, "number 8, clean that shit up." and the man shifted, moving to his dick and licking the cum from his entire rod. He ran his hands up and down the shaft, pumping the rest of his cum out and swallowing it. Jonah put his hand in the man's hair as he cleaned him.

He stepped backward, under the blast of the shower head once again. He let the water run all over him, trying to soap himself up, rinse off, and meet Eve. He thought he was done when he heard yet another woman over the speaker.

"Number seven, grab the wall so that number 10 can fuck you."

This entire thing seemed so surreal. Would this just happen now because some disembodied voice said so? He felt the water on his face as he put his hands up against the wall. Who was number 10? Why was he just going along with this?

Jonah thought about being pegged by Eve. He had been topped before, sure, but it was always with a strapon, by a woman. He had never really even considered this.

He took a deep breath and closed his eyes, leaning his head against the tiles and he felt someone behind him. The man felt bigger than he was, hairier.

He seemed stronger.

Jonah tried to look back but the man pressed his head into the tile, kicking his legs apart. The man grabbed a bar of soap and ran it between Jonah's legs, over his sphincter. He pushed the bar in, pressing it inside of his ass. He kicked his legs apart, almost strong enough to knock him over, then grunted, and pushed his cock directly up his waiting ass.

Jonah breathed in quickly. It felt different than a strap- different than a silicon toy. It was warm and malleable.

And it felt so big.

Jonah let out a little cry when the man pressed him into the wall with a big shove. It felt deep and huge. His feet almost lifted from the ground.

"Number 7, please thank number 10 for fucking you."

He took a deep breath as the rod filled him again and again, twice more. The man seemed to almost pull it completely out before shoving it back in.

"Thank you, thank you for fucking me."

"Number seven, his name is number 10. Can you tell number 10 you love his cock." They laughed.

"Number 10, thank you so much for fucking me, I love your pretty cock so much."

The man seemed turned on by this. He pressed himself deeper inside him and then sped up, fucking into him over and over.

Jonah figured that this might be the way to get it to end sooner.

"Thank you, number 10. I fucking love every part of you fucking me."

The man behind him wrapped his arm around him and fucked harder.

Jonah slammed into the wall so hard he could feel his pelvis click. He pushed his ass backward, trying to follow number 10's rhythm.

Suddenly, Jonah panicked, realizing the man was going to cum inside him. He'd never had anyone cum inside him. He squirmed, but number 10 was too close. He let go and let out a massive noise, pumping white hot cum up Jonah's hole.

That felt like nothing Jonah had ever experienced before. Jonah slid to the ground with the man still inside him. He felt the water on his back as he dipped his head, ass in the air.

And just breathed.

A number of women giggled as the loudspeaker clicked on. "Number 10, piss in the little bitch."

Jonah's eyes widened as he felt himself being filled up like a balloon. Number ten pushed down, preventing him from detaching or getting up. He heard the man behind him whisper, "It's ok. Just take it. You'll be fine. Don't move."

Jonah tried to be calm. It felt wrong. This couldn't be something that he was meant to do. He felt himself fill up, his belly became warm and alien to him. "Please…"

Number ten shushed him and finished. Jonah pulled away finally when he was done and sat on the ground. He looked around for a toilet bowl to evacuate the man's cum and piss. Thankfully, the toilets didn't seem to be surrounded by mirrors.

He moved to stall 20 and cleaned himself quickly before grabbing a towel and stepped out into the room behind the showers. He realized he had forgotten his few articles of clothing as he approached Eve. She was seated nude with a few women around a table filled with fruit and drinks. They were talking and laughing. There were a few men sitting or kneeling on the floor around them.

Jonah looked at her as she pulled him down onto the ground.

She swiveled out and pushed his face into her pussy. He tried to get comfortable on his knees in front of her chair, under the table and he began to suck.

It seemed like there was another load of cum inside her so he went to work, licking and cleaning her. He wondered which of these men had fucked her.

Or was it someone he didn't see.

Every once in a while she repositioned his head the way she wanted. She seemed to forget he was there as he kept sucking on her until she was clean, continuing until she came, softly, into his mouth. He rested his face between her legs, breathing her in.

Jonah had always loved how Eve smelled. Something about the scent of her pussy had always been enough to get him raging hard. One of the things he was realizing he liked about this new, more confident Eve was that he could finally suck her as long as he wanted to. In the past, if he wanted to suck her for too long, she would feel, sometimes, insecure that he didn't want to fuck her.

That he might not like her enough.

The truth was that she was his favorite smell. He wondered, as he rested his head, if they would talk about the other men she had fucked that night or about his experiences in the shower. It all certainly changed the shape of their relationship. In fact, all of this had.

Jonah just didn't know how.

He looked around and saw, next to Eve, the woman Grey, who had tattooed him. She was bottomless, her maroon shirt open at the front. Her skin was so smooth. She had a neatly trimmed shock of black pubic hair. As Jonah considered his two tiny circle tattoos, he saw something. On Grey's inner thigh, in a row, were three diamond shapes. They seemed to be about the same size and color as his circles, around her inner thigh.

And just like that, she crossed her legs and they were gone.

THE YLEROS CONTRACT

Chapter 3

Eve started dressing more provocatively. Jonah loved the new collection of underwear that she had been building, visiting lingerie shops after work. Sometimes he went with her and slipped into the dressing room. He had always loved looking at Eve and the beginning of their relationship was even filled with moments where he felt drab and ordinary next to her.

Eve was tall, only an inch or two shorter than he was, which meant when she wore heels, she could nearly tower over him. She did that rarely, and Jonah worried on occasion that he was forcing her to make herself smaller to accommodate him. Her skin was olive and smooth, from her heart shaped face to her perfect belly, an inheritance from a mixed parentage that she would never know, having been adopted at 3 years old. Her hair was long and dark and fluid, filled with colors that only showed themselves in direct light, but were beautiful nonetheless.

For her part, she was nearly manically attracted to Jonah. His chestnut brown hair made a near perfect ocean wave over a face that was open and inviting, generally smiling. He was one of the only men she had met who could match her intelligence and quick wit and had never once said or done anything to make her feel like she was less of anything.

Eve was planning to ask him to marry her. She had no doubt Jonah would say yes and even less that he would love the feeling of being wanted so much that she would choose a ring and make the first move like that. She had been the one to ask him out in the first place. It was her apartment they had moved into.

Despite all that, Jonah made a good equal for her. And their more and more frequent explorations into power exchange only seemed hot because of that.

They were a good team.

Eve had begun waking him up with a blow job in the morning. Or, on occasion, by sitting on his face. Once he was past the initial surprise, Jonah found that he didn't care which one. He just loved the feeling that they could share that time before he went off to work. Eve worked as a literary critic at a local work collective. Jonah worked in the absolute other direction, as a project manager at a computer security firm. When they kissed goodbye in the morning, They both felt the distance their days would carry them to. More and more, though, they both found their thoughts occupied with the other one.

And it was Eve that Jonah was thinking about at his desk that Monday as he did a casual search on the computer for Yleros. As the search returns came up, though, he was distracted by his head programmer, Keith, brushing by him as he eased into his office.

"What are you doing?"

"Hey. I could have been looking at porn."

Keith laughed. HIs tiny dreads bobbed over his wide face. Keith's infectious smile was familiar in here. He sometimes worked in Jonah's office for some extra privacy. Today, he just brought drinks, though, handing a coffee to Jonah.

"You weren't. You didn't have that 'I'm looking at porn' look on your face."

"Do I have that look?"

Keith took a sip and leaned into the computer. "Sometimes. I've seen it. You doing a sorting exercise?"

Jonah looked at him. "Hm?"

Keith pointed. "Yleros. It's programmer talk for a reverse sort. It's 'sorely' backward. Kind of a programming experiment."

"No. Eve and I have been going to this club and that's the name."

"Ooh. A programmer's club?" Keith winked at him and slid into the chair next to his desk. It was mostly Keith's chair. And he knew most everything about their relationship experiments. Keith wasn't judgmental.

"No. It's like..." Jonah stood up and walked over to the door, closing it. It provided little privacy, really, as his office walls were entirely made of glass. But the sounds of the outer office were muted. He moved back over and sat on his wide desk.

"It's like a sex club where women are in charge. Men do whatever the women want."

"Ok, that's hot."

He rolled up his sleeve and showed Keith his wrist. "And every time we go, I have to get a little tattoo. These.

Keith looked. The two tiny circles were small enough that they could have been freckles. "That's heavy. What happens when your wrist is all filled up?"

Jonah hadn't considered that. At a certain point, they would totally encircle his wrist.

If they went there enough.

And then what? The other wrist? Or another row. For a second, Jonah was hit with a small wave of panic. This was happening on his body and he had no say about it.

Jonah shook his head. "I don't know. This woman named Grey tattoos on me when I go.

Keith laughed. "Grey? Like Grey Shirra-Austen?"

Jonah looked confused, "Who is that?

"Grey Shirra-Austen? The client? The Darpa Client who is in all week?"

"No. No. It's someone different. A blonde woman?"

Keith slid behind his computer, 'Yeah, it's not a super common name, Jo. Here." he flipped the screen around. Jonah could see Grey, in a dark green suit, standing in front of a room full of men. Sure enough, it was her.

"Sonofabitch." Jonah stared.

***

Eve beat him home that night. He found her bottomless in the living room in a small black cropped t-shirt. She was wearing her boots with tall socks. This was one of the outfits she used to ensure Jonah couldn't think straight. And it worked every time.

"Goddamn." He wrapped his arms around her.

She smiled at him. "Do you want some food?"

"Yeah, not right now." He sat down on the couch and she slid to the ground and crawled over to him. He thought he could smell her. "Did you know that Grey is like my boss' boss' boss' boss? Like a few steps added, maybe?"

She put her face in his lap. Jonah could see her ass in the mirror across the room. Two perfect round globes dipping into a darker center. Eve's lips and nipples were close to the same color, almost a rich maroon purple. They were so pretty on her skin, which had a slight reddish tone he could never place. She was magnificent from all angles. Jonah found his cock rising under the heat of her breath. "She works for the government, right?"

"For Darpa, whom we basically work for."

Eve pulled his pants down, along with his underwear, slipping his half erect cock into her mouth.

She loved it when he wasn't totally hard so she could feel him grow in her mouth.

"That's cool. Did you see her at work?"

Jonah lifted his ass and let her pull his clothing all the way off. "If I go to the other side of the office, she'll see me."

"That's hot. I want to see the look on her face."

"Did you know?" Jonah realized he didn't care much as he let his hand drop onto the top of her head. She sucked at him harder, letting his now fully erect dick to fill her mouth.

"I knew she worked for the government. Are you going to listen to the boss?"

"At work?" Jonah laughed. He suddenly realized how weird and hot it all was.

"Do you want to beat me for not telling you?" Eve put one hand on his balls and one on his ass, pulling his prick in and out of her wet open mouth"

"I want to punish you then fuck that ass."

"So you don't need my pussy?" She licked at the little hole at the top of his shaft, trying to get her tongue in it.

"Not tonight, baby." Jonah was hypnotized by the feel of her, the sound of her, the smell of her.

She shot up and ran into the other room. Jonah sat up on the couch. Just as quickly, she returned with a pair of his boots. She kneeled down and kissed his feet, taking his toes in her mouth. It was warm and soft. She opened up two white socks, sliding them onto his feet one at a time. Then, lifting his right boot, she licked the bottom of it, again and again, seemingly cleaning it for him.

This was only the second time they had done this but Jonah knew what came next.

She pulled the boot on as he watched, tying it perfectly. Then, looking like she might have missed a spot, she let her tongue run over the bottom. Jonah grabbed her hair and pushed the tip of the boot in her mouth. Her arms dropped to her sides and she focused, opening as wide as possible as the boot tip split her face. Her mouth seemed to stretch impossibly wide until she coughed and spit up. Jonah pulled the boot out and lifted his other foot.

She repeated her ritual for the other boot, licking the bottom and taking it in her mouth as deeply as she could. He saw her face turn red as she tried to pull it in even deeper until, finally, she nearly threw up. She laughed and then pulled her shirt off.

Her breasts were perfectly teardrop shaped and tipped with the same brilliant velvety color as the skin between her legs. She climbed up and sat next to him, spreading her legs. "Are you sure you don't need my pussy?"

He reached down and dipped his fingers inside her, slipping past her cunt lips. She was slick and wet and warm. He dug out as much of her juices as he could and lifted his fingers to his lips. Sucking them clean, he shook his head.

She looked a tiny bit scared. Jonah wasn't sure if it was real or some affectation for his benefit, meant to make him feel more powerful. She fingered her clit. "Ok, if you don't need it, let's fuck it up."

She slid to the ground and crawled away, looking directly at the far mirror. She spread her legs and lifted her ass. Jonah could see her eyes in the mirror and her tried to keep eye contact as he slipped behind her and pulled back his right leg. He snapped his leg forward and dug the flat top of the boot into her cunt. She let out a little moan and almost fell forward.

Eve tried to adjust her breathing. "Ok. I got it. Ok." She settled herself, calling out, "one."

He pulled his leg back and kicked again, just as hard.

This time she was prepared. "Sorry. Ready."

He let loose, kicking her again, hard, in the vulva.

She called out, "Two." and shifted a little.

The next few came quickly, one after another. The impacts were wet and sloppy sounding, with Eve's open cunt dripping onto the floor, splattering all over his boots.

She called out, "three, four, five, six, seven, eight, nine, ten."

She stared at him defiantly in the mirror, breathing heavily. There was a tear running down her face. "More. Fuck it up. Fifty."

He looked down at her pussy and could see it already swelling up. She looked red and raw. He stepped back and tried to channel all his power. He heard her voice, small, trying to fill the room.

"Eleven, twelve, thirteen fourteen, fifteen, sixteen, seventeen"

He stopped for a moment, reaching down. Her cunt was on fire. It felt so red and raw and hot. She rocked back and forth

"Don't stop, sir, don't stop." She was visibly shaking as he continued. He felt like a monster. So he tried to live in it.

To experience it.

He pulled back again and kicked as hard as he could.

"Eighteen, nineteen, twenty, twentyone, twentytwo, twentythree, twenty four, twenty five."

His boots were slick with her. He looked at her fae in the mirror and could see it was a mess. Her nose was running and tears were splattered all over her face. She was slobbering and he could barely understand her.

"Half...halfway. Please don't stop." Her arms gave out and she let her head fall to the ground. She dug her face into the floorboards. A small pool gathered under her as urine ran down her legs.

Jonah pulled back and slammed his boot into her over and over again.

"Twenty six, twenty seven, twenty eight, twenty nine, thirty, thirty one, thirty two thirty three."

She was sobbing now, loudly. But panicking that he had stopped. "Don't stop. Don't. Please baby. Fuck my pussy up.

Piss streamed out of her as her belly trembled. He began kicking again.

"Thirty four, thirty five, thirty six, thirty seven, thirty eight, thirty nine, FORTY." She called out, buckling over and collapsing in foetal position on the floor.

Jonah leaned down and held her hand. Are you ok, baby?"

She nodded.

He kissed her, feeling the slimy mess that was her face. He licked at her lips, tasting all of her, every fluid of her. "Let's stop, sweetheart."

She broke down, crying harder, "Don't stop, don't stop, don't stop." She grabbed him, kissing him. Then she laid back down on her back. Jonah ran his hand over her pussy. It was completely discolored. He could see his bootprints on her belly, where he had missed, and they were slowly turning black and blue. She lifted her arms and spread her legs.

10 more.

He stood up and moved up her body, placing his right foot right above her pussy. She spread her legs as he positioned his boot on the split in her legs. He pulled back and kicked again.

"Forty one, forty two, forty three, forty four, forty five, forty six, forty seven."

She stared up, immobile. She refused to close her legs or protect herself. He kicked three more final times.

"Forty eight, forty nine, fifty."

She rolled over shaking. He laid down next to her, sinking into the pool of urine on the floor, holding her. Her body was racked in sobs. "I'm sorry I fucked all those guys at the club without talking about it. I should have talked to you about it. I'm sorry, I'm sorry."

He petted her hair, "It's okay, baby, we're experimenting. I got your back, it's all right. You know some guy fucked me."

She let out a quick laugh through the sobs, "Really?"

"Yep. He fucked me then pissed in my ass."

Her breathing slowed a little, "You got your cherry popped and I missed it?"

"Yep. First man cock inside me and you missed it."

"Damn."

"How does your pussy feel?"

"It hurts so bad. I don't think I'll ever touch it again." she laughed a little. "Are you still going to screw my ass?"

Jonah nodded and kissed her. They were covered in her piss. He slid down her body licking it off of her. As he reached her midsection, he lifted her legs and slid in, pulling her ass up. Her pussy juices had drenched the space between her asscheeks, making it easy for him to just slide his cock in . He heard her sharply breath in as he started to fuck her.

He tried to avoid her ruined pussy as he dug his rod deeply into her ass, pushing harder and harder with each thrust. She wrapped her legs around him, the pool of cold piss under them making splashing noises with every downward movement.

Jonah lifted his hand to her face, inserting three fingers into her mouth. She pulled them in, letting him facefuck her with his hand. Her lips stretched open widely again as he slowly moved the hand deeper down her throat.

She was choking now but she had put one of her hands on his now, trying to fuck her own mouth with his hand, pushing it down her gullet as hard as she could.

She began spitting up just as Jonah let loose, cumming up her ass. He came in waves, each one more intense than the one before. He stayed there for a minute, letting his hand marinate in her mouth. He could feel his fingers crossing the tiny sphincter in the back of her throat. He put his other hand in her hair and pressed, until the finger slipped deeper inside. For a second, Eve seemed to panic until she started swallowing, pulling his finger further down her throat. She pushed his hand down, trying to get the knuckles past the opening of her mouth. He started moving, fucking the hole in the back of her throat. She dropped her arms and let him, trying so hard to take it until she coughed and started vomiting. He turned her on her side as she finished, wiping her face.

She was shaking. Suddenly, it seemed cold in the room. She was wet. He grabbed a blanket from the couch and wrapped her up, lifting her off hte ground and carrying her into the bathroom. 10 minutes later, she was in a warm bath with her head leaning back against their inflatable tub pillow.

***

Jonah carried the last of the candles into the bathroom, placing them around the edge of the tub.

"How are you feeling?" He petted her hair. She was still a mess.

"Ohmigod. This feels good. I think I fucked four guys at the club? Two came in me."

"I know. I ate that out of you."

She smiled and caressed his face. "You did, you were so good. One of them, I slapped his face until he was bleeding. He couldn't cum. I was mean."

"So mean." Jonah did that thing that men do where he made sure her breasts were extremely clean with his hands under the bubbles.

"Did you know that Grey worked for the government?"

"I did. She told me when she reached out to me."

Jonah was confused, "ok, backtrack. I don't understand."

Eve stuck her breasts out for his ministrations. "The erotica I write. On the message boards? She saw some and asked if I wanted to join."

"Just like that?"

"Just like that. And she told me where she worked."

Jonah sighed. "Ok."

Eve scrunched up her face. "Hey. Why don't you just talk to her. At work. Go see her."

"Just like that?"

Eve laughed. "Yes, again, just like that."

He smiled and washed her hair. She sunk under the water for a second and then came back up.

"Just remember to do exactly what she says, no matter what."

THE YLEROS CONTRACT

Chapter 4

Jonah went into work the next day and worked with Keith in his office for the first part of the day. As they split for lunch, he played a hunch.

Opening the company directory, he looked for his own name. Jonah Gilden. A picture of him popped up on the screen, one he immediately downloaded.

Then he searched wider, through clients as well, for Grey Shirra-Austen.

Her picture and contact information appeared. He stared at it. She was an attractive woman, Her picture here seemed more relaxed. He tried to reconcile that with the stern woman he knew.

But, honestly, he didn't know her at all. He thought for a second and then clicked the contact link. An email window opened up.

To: GreyShirra-Austen@DARPA.gov

Subject: Can we talk

Body: Hello. This is Jonah Gilden. I have enclosed a picture. Could we speak today?

He attached the picture and quickly hit send. Suddenly, he was terrified. What did he just do. This woman was many times over his boss. He heard a notification bing and clicked at the top of the screen. She had responded.

RE: Can we talk

Body: Be in my office at 6 pm. East wing. Corridor A.

She had made an appointment. She wanted to see him.

He wasted a good part of the rest of the day. It was hard to think about anything but this. Although he still had no idea what he was going to ask.

Not really any at all.

At 5:45 he made his way to the East wing. He moved down corridor A, wondering if he was going to be able to find the office. The entire space was huge. It turned out it wasn't hard at all.

Her office was the only one in corridor A. He waited a few minutes until it was precisely 6, opening the thick wooden door into a library-like space. Unlike his office and the rest in the West area, these were all wooden, built out under high ceilings with massive book filled bookshelves.

There was a small, attractive, upscale looking black woman sitting behind the desk in an impeccable white suit. She looked up at him as he approached, hitting a button on the phone. A woman's voice came from the phone "thank you." and she waved him toward the inner door.

Jonah opened it and walked in. Grey was standing in front of her desk with her arms crossed. He pulled the door shut behind him and walked toward her.

She nodded at him. "Jonah Gilden."

He breathed out. "You..You know who I am?"

Grey moved to sit behind her desk. "I do."

Jonah looked around. There were no chairs. "I wasn't sure if you were allowed to talk to me here."

Grey smiled, "I'm allowed to do anything I like. Now, remove your clothes."

Jonah hadn't expected that. "I'm sorry. You want me to…"

"Jonah."

She closed a folder and slid it into a manilla envelope, snapping her fingers at him.

He started taking his clothes off, starting with his shirt and working down. He tried to fold them but there was no surface to place them on but the floor. He stopped when he reached his underwear. He wore blue striped boxers.

She looked at him without speaking.

He put his thumbs in the waistband and pulled them down.

Grey stared at him for a minute. He realized that she might have been concerned he had a listening device.

He did not.

She pushed a button on the phone. "Marissa, can you come in here?"

The receptionist in front entered, closing the door behind her. She was quick.

"Could you please properly fold Jonah Gilden's clothes and hold on to them at your desk?"

Marissa seemed unphased. "Of course." She moved into the room and picked up Jonah's clothes. She held them in her arms. Jonah tried not to cover himself or act embarrassed. No one else seemed to think this was out of the ordinary.

"Do you need anything else, Ms Shirra-Austen?"

She stood up, "Marissa, could you help Jonah climb up on the desk?"

Marissa nodded and grabbed Jonah's arm, pulling him to the desk. She helped him climb up and stay there on his hands and knees.

"Thank you, dear. Give me thirty minutes."

"Yes, ma'am. Jonah was keenly aware of her stare as she left the room, closing the door loudly.

Jonah was cold. But more than that, he felt awkward. He had no idea how he was supposed to talk or behave. "I was hoping to ask some questions."

Grey Shirra-Austen pulled a giant container of coconut oil from the cabinet behind her. "You can ask, sure. Now, spread your legs."

He spread his legs and lifted his ass in the air. She pulled on a black rubber glove and grabbed a handful of coconut oil, layering it into his ass. With her other hand she held onto his cock, dipping down between his legs.

She placed her gloved hand at the entrance of his ass. "Breath in deep. Now exhale." She pushed her hand into him. Jonah had never been fisted and wasn't sure it was possible. She pressed her hand expertly into the puckering hole in his ass, slowly letting it open.

"Breathe in again. Now open your ass."

He did. He heard a slight pop as her fist slid inside him. His prick was half erect between his legs as she slowly massaged it while feeling around inside him. For a moment, he remembered that Eve had told him to do whatever Grey had said. His cock twitched at the thought that he was making Eve happy by behaving.

Grey began to milk him. He felt her fingers on his prostate as a slow drip of cum started falling from his cock. It was a strange feeling. In a way it was orgasmic, but slower.

"What did you want to ask me, Jonah Gilden?"

He was breathing heavily now, feeling the weight of the orgasm that wouldn't stop. "What are the diamond tattoos on your thigh from?"

She laughed. "Press the red button."

He reached over on the phone and pressed the red button.

Marissa's voice rang out. "Yes?"

Grey took a beat. "Could you be a dear and bring in the A Package?"

Marissa asked, "just one?"

Grey Shirra-Austen responded, "Yes, sweetheart, just the one"

Marissa signed off, "Yes Sir."

Grey yanked at Jonah's cock. "See? She knows enough to call me 'sir'"

He shot back, "Yes, sir."

Marissa came in, again closing the door behind her. "It's in his pocket, in his pants, folded in the corridor."

Grey had a smile in her voice. "Thank you my, dear. How is the form here?"

Marissa looked at Jonah. He tried to avoid her gaze. "His back should be arched a bit more, maybe?"

Grey nodded, "I agree. Is he a good cow?"

Marissa laughed, "Maybe with a lot of practice, but sure."

Grey squeezed his prick as the last of his cum came spilling out. It was a bizarre feeling for Jonah, like nothing he'd ever experienced. He realized that Marissa being a secretary made all this even more humiliating. He vowed to explore that. Was he a classist?

"Would you want to do this next time, if he comes to see me again?"

Marissa nodded, "I could try. You're better, but I think I could. My hands are smaller, though."

"Ok. If he comes back, do what you need to. Then I'll talk to him."

"Thank you, sir." Marissa slipped out of the office.

Grey slapped his ass. "Now breathe out."

He did, and he felt her hand pop as it pulled out of him. "Your clothes are in the corridor outside. Get cleaned up. 9pm tonight."

Jonah climbed down from the table. The room was spinning around. "Thank you, sir." He looked at her and she waved him out, cleaning up her desk.

He walked out into Marissa's office outside, unsteadily. She looked up at him from her desk, "Do you need help, Jonah?"

He shook his head, moving toward the door. He avoided her eyes.

"I'll see you soon, Jonah." She kept using his name in such a way that it reinforced her familiarity. The easy she said it meant she had power over him.

"Thank you." He opened the door, still naked.

"Thank you, sir." she asserted.

Jonah looked at the receptionist. He felt an overwhelming wave of something. He couldn't place it. He walked to her desk. He dropped his head. "I'm sorry, sir."

Mariss smiled, "ok. Go." she nodded to the door.

He stepped out of her office into a corridor he was afraid would be full of life. It was empty and dark. He looked down to see his clothes, neatly folded. He pulled the pants on and his t-shirt and started walking back to the western most wing of the building.

Back in his office, he started to come alive. He had a small private shower in his bathroom. He stripped and stepped under the spray of water. It was nearly 8:00 and he remembered she had said 9pm. His ass hurt less than he thought it would. He scrubbed it, not knowing what the rest of the night would bring.

He dried off and pulled his clothes back on. In his pocket was a small, business card sized envelope. It was black, with the capital letter "A" on it. On one side was a silver inscription - an address.

In the envelope was a black key, exactly like the one Eve had, but instead of the "y" it held an "A".

It was a different club.

He pulled his phone out and texted EVE

Grey sent me to a different club tonight at 9. Be home after.

He immediately saw the dots as she started typing. Her response only took a minute or so.

See you at home later. Make sure you do what she says.

The way she typed that reminded Jonah, again, that he felt she knew something he didn't. He shrugged. Maybe there would be some answers tonight.

***

He pulled into the parking lot at the address. There weren't any cars. It was a Tuesday night, so he didn't expect much.

He saw the sign, a stylized capital "A" and walked toward it. As he approached, he saw a pretty girl with short dark hair dressed in a sheer dress. She walked up to him.

"Jonah Gilden?"

He looked at her. "Yes, are you supposed to meet me?"

She smiled, "I'm with you tonight."

She was thin, slight. Much smaller than Eve. But she was very pretty. She just looked a bit fragile. She didn't seem dominant at all. She shook Jonah's hand. "I'm Giselle."

"It's good to meet you. Have you been here?"

She nodded. She pulled up her dress to show me a row of 7 or so small diamonds tattooed on her inner thigh. Her pussy was shaved completely and was bright pink. he nodded. These were the same diamonds that Grey had tattooed on her.

He held out his arm for her and tried to pretend he'd been here. Stepping through the door, they found themselves in a small black foyer area very similar to Yleros. He looked at Giselle. Pulling out the key, He opened the door.

The inner foyer was wide and dark, lit with blue lights that seemed to swim around the room. He looked to his right to see a table, similar to the Yleros, with a large brooding black man in a suit behind it. As he stepped in, he smiled and reached his hand out, "Mr. Gilden, Good to see you."

He nodded and took his hand. Jonah tried to imagine if he'd seen him before. Giselle, next to him, started removing her dress and shoes, folding them and placing them on the table.

The man let go of his hand. "I'm Gerald. It's good to meet you. Welcome to Archon" He reached over and grabbed Giselle by the arm and dragged her onto the table, nude. He reached in with his right hand and deftly inserted his thumb in her asshole as he cupped her ass, holding her down. With his left hand he pushed her head down roughly so that she was lying flat.

"Check out the rules here, and I hope you have a great time, Mr. Gilden." He pulled out a small tattoo gun and positioned it next to the small row of diamonds on her inner thigh, adding one. He was rough and unyielding with her and Jonah could see her trying hard not to squirm. Just as Grey seemed to have no interest in talking to men, Gerald had no desire, seemingly, to speak to women.

He looked up at the rules behind him on the board. They were familiar.

1. Women will not wear clothing of any kind

2. Women will not speak unless explicitly asked to

3. Women will be prepared to serve with all of their holes, at the demand of men

4. Women will not look men directly in the eye

5. Women will bring men drinks and whatever they need

6. Women will respond enthusiastically at all times

7. Women will be free to use if they are alone

8. Women will be available to be taken upstairs if they are alone

9. Women will point to or bring to men tools they wish to be beaten with

10. Women will not speak to each other.

He tried to remember the exact rules at Yleros. These seemed slightly more severe. Or were they.

Did it seem that way because they were women?

Gerald slapped Giselle hard on the ass when he was done, pulling his thumb from her asshole. She slid off the table next to me, looking about 20 times more submissive than she had outside. Her head was down. He still didn't really understand the tattoos but it was clear that only the submissives got them. And an additional one each time they came. It looked like this was her 8th time here. He looked her over and saw a row of three star tattoos along her spine. I whispered to her, "What are these from?"

She whispered back. "Those are from Madara. It's a different club."

Jonah nodded. "And this place is called 'Archon'?"

She looked into my eyes and responded, "yes."

He pulled her into the main room beyond. There were about a hundred people there, on a Tuesday. Most of them were couples, but there were occasional men or women on their own wandering around.

Right in front of him was a pool table where four men were playing pool bottomless while about six women tried to keep up, sucking their cocks and asses as they set up shots. The men seemed to not notice the women at all.

He watched for a second, hypnotized. A taller man, dark and swarthy, was lining up a shot while a blonde woman sucked enthusiastically on his prick, her arms wrapped around a dark haired woman behind him, her face buried deeply in his ass. He stopped for a moment, lifting his head.

Jonah could tell he was near orgasm and was holding on as long as he could. The blond woman was shoving the other woman's face deeply into the opening in his ass as she held his balls and pressed her face deeply onto his shaft, nearly choking. He yelled out, "ooooh, fuck." and came into her mouth violently. He nearly fell against the table and Jonah saw the balls shake a bit. The game seemed built around the attention the women provided. The men laughed.

Jonah looked at Giselle and saw how pretty she really was. He put his hand between her legs, slapping them apart. She spread them widely and leaned against the table behind them. She was wet and open with a surprisingly wide bare pussy. He slid his hand into it and his other hand around her neck. She was so small that he could lift her and hold her against the wall. This was something he could never do with Eve.

He felt her slide down his hand as it rode up inside her. She breathed in sharply at the sound of his hand lodging itself in her open cunt. He squeezed from the sides on her neck, watching her arms go limp. Her body weight rested on his hand, exploring her cunt as he leaned in to kiss her. He kissed her warmly, excited by the realization that he could do anything he wanted here.

Anything

Suddenly he felt that surge that Eve must have felt at Yleros.

Anything he wanted.

He kissed her harder, Slamming her against the wall as he pumped his hand in her. Her mouth was wet and open and her lips conformed perfectly to his. He found her little button inside and began to tap in rhythmically pushing up. He pressed himself against her, pushing her belly in with his body until he could feel his own hand through her skin. She moaned and tried to rub herself against him, but she had no leverage. He pulled his mouth back and spit in her mouth. She opened wide, swallowing his spit and resuming kissing him.

He felt her back slam into the wall again and again as he rhythmically fist fucked her and pushed her back and forth with his hand wrapped tightly around her neck. Her arms lay there, useless. Jonah realized she had never even considered fighting back.

He pushed in and out with greater intensity as she moaned louder, her pussy dripping down her legs. As she got closer, he leaned in, holding her weight up by her neck. He slammed his fingers in her clit over and over until he felt the familiar quiver and pulled them out quickly, letting her squirt all over the floor as she hung there by her neck in his hands. She reached up now, with both hands on his hand, kicking her legs until the spray abated.

He slowly slid her down the wall until she was kneeling at his feet. He pulled his cock out and pointed it at her. She opened her mouth in front of him, her hands on his legs, waiting as he let go, pissing into her open mouth. She tried to catch it all, but some of his piss joined her juices on the floor in a mess that needed to be cleaned up.

Jonah kneeled down and pressed her face on the wet floor. She began to lick up the liquid that had fallen everywhere. He pulled her ass up as she did, plunging his now-erect dick into her from behind.

He came in her for the first time that night. And as the evening progressed, he was able to fill her two more times. He beat her, fucked her, and facefucked her and a number of other women across the club that night. And by the time he was done, he knew exactly how Eve had felt and why it was changing her every day. She felt like a goddess. She felt invincible.

At 2am, he stepped out of the club with a wet and disheveled Giselle. She left her clothes inside and followed him, carrying only her slight purse, sitting next to him in the passenger seat with her legs spread. He realized that her tiny frame created the illusion that her pussy was big and meaty and wide open. It made him want to explore it. He reached in the back seat and found a thick travel cup that he had earlier filled with coffee. It was smooth and tall.

"I like how big and sloppy your pussy is."

She looked down and spread wider. "Thank you, sir."

"I want you to sit on this on the way home." He placed the travel mug on the seat in front of her.

She looked at him. "My pussy or my ass, sir."

"Can you get it in your cunt?"

She nodded. She spit on it, trying to lubricate it. She rubbed it in and lifted herself up, placing the cup below her. She pulled the lips of her cunt apart and settled on top of it. Her vagina was so bare and pink it seemed that Jonah could easily see it as it slipped into her. She let out a low moan as she let herself slide down it until she was seated again, on the seat. Her breathing became shallower while she tried to accommodate the object inside her.

"Are you ok?" he asked, putting his hand on her hair. It was still wet from the hours of play.

She nodded, but kept breathing hard. It was clear she could feel it inside her.

Jonah laughed as he drove her home, making sure to hit every bump he could. She seemed to feel them all so intensely. He told her to masturbate and watched her squirt across his seat, twice.

They stopped in front of her house. "Give me my cup back." Jonah held out his hand. She lifted herself up and dug the base of it out of her, pulling until it slid all the way out.

She handed it to him, holding onto her cunt tightly.

"Is that ok?" He asked again.

She nodded. "I'm just. I had fun, sir."

He leaned in and kissed her. Suddenly, he felt that strange power. It was overwhelming. "Do you have an extra key?"

She nodded her head, fishing through her bag. She pulled it out. It was a pink metal key covered in stars. She held it out to him.

He took it, opening the glove compartment to place it inside and pulled out a pad of paper and a pen. "Here, write down your apartment number and phone number."

She looked at him for a minute and wrote on the pad.

She looked both ways before opening the door and running out. Her ass shook as she made her way to the door and ducked inside.

He texted her on his phone and thought for a second. He licked the travel cup in his hand. It tested pink and amazing. It was warm.

He looked down at his phone and saw it light up.

I'm safe inside. I'm here every night after 7, sir.

And he couldn't wait to get home.

Chapter 5

Eve was awake when he got home, wearing only her tall knit socks. Since they had been going to Yleros, she had been wearing less and less around the house. Jonah had always loved her body. She was slightly curvy, in ways that made a simple pair of shorts into something pornographic. Her breasts were thick and full and when she bent over, it was a miraculous thing. As far as Jonah was concerned, the more she was naked, the better. And the stocking made it seem even dirtier.

He flopped down on the couch to tell her everything that had happened. He showed her his key with the letter "A" on it. As he looked at her, he realized she had started wearing the Yleros key around her neck. And as they talked, she touched it frequently.

She touched it when she was turned on.

She slid down and filled her mouth with his dick as he talked. He told her about Giselle, about Gerald, about the pool match he had observed. Through it all. She pumped at his prick with her mouth, aggressively, as though it were hers. He told her about Grey and the events of the day, about Marissa, about all of it.

She sucked at him, playing with his balls. She pushed him back on the couch and lifted his legs, digging her face into his ass while she jacked his cock. He tried to focus on the story but soon found it nearly impossible. Suddenly, he felt the warm rush and came all over his belly. She smiled and ran her tongue up his dick and across the area, licking it all up.

They laughed together on the couch.

He could see her ass on the surfce of it as she straddled it, still with her face between his legs. She nibbled at his balls.

"How many times have you cum today, now?"

Jonah tried to think. It was a lot. "Five? Or, wait... six?"

Eve looked up at him and knelt on the floor. "Can we play a game?"

He nodded. "Sure." He slid down the couch and joined her on the floor.

"ok. " she kissed him. "I'm horny and I want to be fucked."

Jonah looked at her and cocked his head. "Ok. So..."

She looked at him demurely,"You play with your cock and try to get hard again so you can take care of my needs. If you can't get it up, I beat you until you can."

The sound of her voice alone was making him think he could do it. He felt his prick twitch. Then he saw it.

She was literally fondling the key. It turned her on so much that she was caressing it.

He nodded. "Ok. Here goes." He started rubbing his dick. She shot up and ran out of the room. Watching her beautiful ass shake up and down as she ran brought him to at least half mast. He pulled at his prick, slowly, trying not to rush it.

She stepped back in the room brandishing a belt. There were little strings of liquid between her thighs, showing him how excited she was just holding the belt. She slapped it against itself.

"C'mon, baby. I want to get laid." She waved the belt at him as he jacked a little harder, breathing in.

She stepped up to him and dug her fingers into her pussy, placing them in his mouth. "Don't you want my holes, baby? Don't you think I'm hot?" She snapped the belt again.

He nodded up and down and realized he'd pushed a bit too hard. He let go of his dick and let it swing for a second. He reached for her.

"What the fuck are you doing?" She folded the belt and swung it, hitting him hard in the chest. It hurt. She put her hand on his throat. "Do you want me to help?"

She squeezed and choked him. He felt his dick move a little as he put his hand between his legs, trying again to get it hard. She hit him across the chest again with the belt. And twice more in rapid succession.

Jonah's nipples were hot and stinging. She had never whipped him with a belt like that. He looked down and tried harder to get erect.

"I work so hard to be ready for you and I suck you and i let you punt me in the cunt and everything you want and now you can't even get fucking hard for me." She pulled back and just began slamming the belt into him, across his chest and back. He felt the welts rise as he worked his rod.

He wasn't getting hard.

She pushed him down on the ground and pulled back the belt. Again and again it came down on him all over. She hit him between the legs and a white hot pain exploded everywhere. He put his hands up to protect himself.

"Drop your fucking hands, drop them." She began breathing harder as she hit him over and over again with the looped belt, across the chest, stomach, even on his cock and legs. He let his arms drop to the sides as he just took it . He rolled over into a foetal position while the belt came slapping down on his skin over and over again. He stopped trying and just let go letting her beat him all across his body. He thought about the entire night and how much he had enjoyed it, about Giselle, about all of it as he began to cry in pain.

She didn't stop.

He thought about how he had kicked at her pussy less than 48 hours ago, leaving marks that still shone through on her upper belly.

He flattened himself on the floor and let her beat him.

"But you don't think about me, about how I might need some cock and I might want to get laid and feel good. You came over and over today, never once thinking that I might want to cum and feel loved and feel all of your load in my belly. And that's how you love someone who would do anything for you, someone you won't even get your dick hard for."

Jonah was crying, his face digging into the floor, trying to feel every belt mark, every one he deserved. She was screaming, bringing the belt down over and over. Suddenly she stopped.

Jonah was flat on the ground, tears pouring out of his eyes. "I'm sorry, I'm sorry, I'm sorry..."

Eve pulled a blanket over and curled up next to him. She covered them both and kissed his face. He turned and pressed his head into her neck. She pulled his hair back off his face.

"Do you still love me?"

Jonah nodded silently, opening his mouth for her kiss.

They fell asleep on the floor with their mouths open, connected, kissing.

***

The next morning, Eve joined him in the shower, wearing a strap on. He played along, pretending she was a man, massaging her cock. They made out under the spray of water. His skin still hurt and the welts from the belt were everywhere. She kissed his neck and back and slowly pushed him against the wall, her cock rubbing up against his ass. And she seemed to get hornier and hornier the more it did.

Jonah put his hands behind him and spread his ass, opening it for her.

She put the head of the dildo and placed it right at the entrance of his ass and pushed, holding his hips. He sank backwards onto it and let it fill him up. She slid in and out as the water fell on both of them. Jonah slowly stroked his dick as she did, trying to match her rhythm

For a second, he thought about how much he loved fucking her. How turned on he was sliding his cock inside Eve. It was exciting to him to think that she might think the same way about him. When she bent over, he couldn't think straight.

Was she feeling that about him?

That would be amazing. He thought about that and increased his rhythm. He poured conditioner in his hand to prevent his dick from chafing from the water. And when he finally came, after three massive thrusts from Eve, he held his hand out, capturing his load in his left hand. He turned to her and kissed her. He pressed his left hand against her ass and wiped his cum all over it, pushing it inside with his fingers. She spread her legs and took it in. She reached up and pulled a buttplug from the shower shelf and inserted it inside her.

He kissed her. She wanted him inside her all day today.

Their lips opened and closed, connecting.

Jonah realized the shower lasted nearly three times longer than his others and smiled.

As he got dressed, she kissed his marks, stepping out to get to work. He looked down ot the dresser. She had placed his key right where he could grab it. And next to it, the piece of paper with Giselle's information.

He chuckled and put them in his pocket.

In the car, he checked for everything he needed. He pulled his phone out and sawGiselle's message. On a whim, he texted her:

Send me a picture.

Nearly immediately, he saw the dots. She responded with a picture.

It was obviously shot in a car. She had pulled her dress up and spread the lips of her pussy. In the picture, he could see her open cunt and the slight belly above it. Her frame seemed impossibly small for that pretty, wide open pussy.

He texted back:

Archon. Day after tomorrow. 9pm.

She texted in response, nearly immediately:

Yes, sir.

Those two words were impossibly hot.

His skin felt hot and tight as he sat, driving to work. But he felt loved. In fact, it had been a long time since he had felt this loved. From all sides.

That lasted until he got to his office. Marissa was sitting in the chair in front of his desk. She had unlocked his office and let herself in.

He made his way to his chair and sat down. "Hello."

Marissa looked up. "Shh." She pulled a card out of her jacket pocket and held it up. "Eyes down, Jonah."

He looked down, focusing on her feet. She placed the card on his desk. "I am having a party for friends tonight. It starts at 8. You will be there at 7. Eyes down, no talking, no clothes, no attitude. Answer yes if you understand."

He took a breath. All he could do was answer. "Yes."

She stood up. "You will get a pip for it."

He must have looked confused because she pointed to his wrist. "One pip"

She turned and walked out of his office as Keith stepped in. They watched her walk toward the East Wing of the building.

Keith looked at him. "Should I ask what that was about?"

Jonah shrugged. I am not 100% sure I can explain it." He pulled his phone out and typed to Eve.

Grey's secretary says I have to be at her party tonight

He waited. Just as he was about to put the phone back in his pocket, she responded:

Do what they say.

He looked over at Keith, who was already sitting down at the desk, getting ready to work.

He continued typing to Eve:

Day after tomorrow, I'm meeting Giselle again at Archon. Do you want to come?

Jonah moved back to his desk and sat, placing the phone next to him. Just as he was about to start, his notification went off. It was Eve:

Yes. I do. I'm excited.

Jonah wasn't 100% sure he was allowed to do that. But then he remembered how Grey had acted about Yleros. She was essentially allowed to do anything she wanted.

Keith put the top of his computer down. "ok , dude. You aren't here at all today. Do you want to talk about it?"

Jonah sat ont ch couch in front of the big open windows. "I do, but I don't know where to start. There are multiple versions of these clubs."

"Ok, different ones?"

Jonah nodded. "at least three different ones"

"So, one where women are in charge?"

"One where men are in charge." Jonah crossed his legs.

Keith looked appreciative, "I like that." he exhaled. "What does Eve think?"

Jonah laughed. "She's so turned on that she's dragging her key everywhere. It's on a chain around her neck."

"Key?"

He reached into his pocket. "Like this one."

Keith took it and stared. "A?"

Jonah nodded, "The club. Archon."

His friend laughed. "Well, that's appropriate. Archon. It's greek for 'ruler.' What's the third?"

He thought. "Hm. It's Madara, I think?"

"Ok. well, that's Hausa for 'Milk'"

Jonah stared at him. "How are you language guy, all of a sudden?"

Keith shook his head, "I'm not. I'm a Nigerian computer programmer who went to a Greek orthodox high school back in the 2030s. You just happened to hand me three words I know, and I appreciate that. Made me look smart as hell."

Jona laughed, "hey, no problem. It's just because I feel like an idiot." He looked out into the main work area. "Does it seem to you like we have fewer people every day?"

"It doesn't just feel that way. People are dropping out of the work force everywhere."

"Well, sometimes I wish I could just drop out." He took the key back from Keith. "Hey, you should come to this place with me sometime."

"I'm not really a massively kinky guy. If they served free food, I'd be there."

"You know, I didn't even look."

They worked in his office for a good part of the day. Toward the end of the day, his phone binged again.

He looked down to see another picture from Giselle. This one was of her face and breasts. It looked like it might have been taken in a clean room—or a hospital. She was staring to the left and her short black hair was in disarray. Her breasts were small and pointed nearly upward. She was really very pretty.

He lifted the phone and smiled, taking a picture and sending it to her in return.

He heart reacted to her shot and put the phone away. The rest of the day was a blur. He looked at the card for Marissa's party. It was across town, so he figured he would leave early. He thought back to how she had spoken to him in his own office and tried to figure out how he felt about it.

Was it hot? Marissa was tiny. She couldn't have been more than 25 and was barely 5 feet tall. Even her voice was slight, little. She was a receptionist. And yet, she commanded him like she was in the military.

The street was empty as he pulled up in front of her place. This was becoming sort of the status quo all over the city. Most people were working from home now and the rest had apparently moved on to greener pastures. The illusion was that the city was emptying out.

The card directed him to the fourth floor. From the shape of the building, Jonah would have guessed that there were 4 or 5 apartments on that floor. But as the elevator opened, he saw that the entire floor had been converted to one apartment. And that looked relatively new.

There was a corridor in front of the elevator and, as he peered down it, he could see Marissa approaching. There was no way this entire place was hers.

Was there?

She was in a red fluffy robe that seemed to have nothing under it. She motioned to him to follow her as she led him into a room where two other men stood naked. Behind a log table was a a woman in a black turtleneck and jeans. Marissa waved to him to step up.

He looked at the other men and saw the tattoos on their wrists. He began to strip off his clothes. Marissa watched him closely, looking impatient. She turned to the other woman. "A pip for him and a Twillerex shot."

He looked up. That was unexpected. Twillerex was a hypo shot developed in 2036 that was meant to prevent pregnancy, STIs, and parasites. Jonah still had a year to go before he needed a new shot.

But he was sure she knew that. This was her way of making him feel dirty, lesser. Taking control.

He stepped up and the woman grabbed his arm roughly, pressing it down on the table. She pulled out a tattoo gun and deftly drew a tiny circle matching the others.

His third.

When that was done, she reached over and grabbed his cock and balls with her left hand. She lifted him onto the table and slapped at his legs.

He spread them.

The woman shook her head noting his welts. "He's a fucking mess."

Marissa laughed. "Good, I like it." She reached over and grabbed his right nippled between her thumb and forefinger twisting hard. Jonah closed his eyes and took it. It was nothing compared to last night.

The woman in the turtleneck Took out a hypo and gave him a shot on his inner thigh. A warm wave shot through him. She kept hold of his cock and balls, using them to slide him back off the table.

At another time, he would have found her incredibly attractive. The woman had wild reddish black hair, with breasts so full they caused her turtleneck to ride up, exposing the bellybutton on a sleek white belly.

She slapped his dick, forcing him to move away from the table. The woman glanced over at Marissa. "That one looked at me. He needs training."

Marissa shook her head, "hell, he looks like he got trained last night."

She slapped him hard on the ass as he averted his eyes. "Jonah, get back on the table."

He turned and climbed back on the table. The woman in the black turtleneck smelled amazing. He closed his eyes as she grabbed him between the legs again. She pushed his head down. He turned to the right and stared. Marissa stepped to the door and let her robe fall. One of the men grabbed it for her. She was completely naked underneath it, talking and laughing with three other naked women in the doorway.

He felt something cold inserted in his ass and realized that the woman he was so attracted to had lubed up his ass and inserted it. His face burned red with humiliation. The cold object seemed to slide deeply inside him, past the point where he could feel it. The woman put her hand on his back pushing down. As he arched his back he could feel how deeply he was impaled. He placed a box in his hand.

"Jonah. This is an obedience test. Are you ready?"

He nodded as he watched the women interact. They looked so free and happy. They looked bigger than life. Marissa's breasts were beautiful. He didn't realize. His cock rode up, pressed against his belly

"Press the button until I say stop."

Jonah pressed the button and a wave of red flashed across his eyes. The rod carried an electrical current deep inside him, past his belly, it seemed. The feeling was intense and hot. It was painful but more than anything it felt wrong. This should not be happening. His cock stayed solidly erect, pressed against him.

"Now let go."

He stopped pushing the button and his vision returned. He looked at the women in the doorway and saw one, someone new.

She was entirely pink. From head to toe.

He tried to see better.

"Press the button, Jonah."

He pressed it again and the electrical wave slashed through his bowels and belly, setting his insides on fire. He heard her laughing and desperately tried to catch the pink woman.

"Now let go."

He let go of the button and it felt amazing. It was as if there was no pain in the world. He breathed in. He could still smell the woman, even as she yanked at his prick to turn him around.

"Press the button, Jonah."

He let out a scream as he pressed it. This one felt worse. She flipped him over, using his balls as a handle, and spread his legs. He realised the electric current was stimulating his prostate. His cock was rock hard as she spread his legs on the table watching his dick convulse as he shot his load into the air.

She laughed. "Now let go."

Jonah was breathing hard. He could feel everyone's eyes on him.

The woman retrieved a wet washcloth and wiped down his dick and balls. She pressed down on his belly and slowly pulled out the device. Jonah took a sharp intake of breath as she slid it out. She slapped him and he climbed off the table. He felt property chastened.

But as he walked out of the room to serve all he could think was "who was that pink woman?"

Chapter 6

Eve Ungaro had been a critic for various literary magazines since she was 20 years old. She was a terse writer when dissecting a novel, functional and not flowery, and her critiques often made it into syndication due to their authenticity and strength. She was incredibly well read, which allowed her to have a scope of narrative experience that added authority to her work.

But that wasn't where her passion was.

It was her own writing.

Shortly after they met, Jonah had learned that she had been writing Femdom BDSM pornography online, as a hobby, for years, under the pen name "Jocasta." And people loved what she wrote. Her fans were really engaged, writing letters, sharing her work. There had even been talk of a book deal, before the economy had slowed. They loved her.

Because she had ideas.

Jonah imagined that this was why she was blossoming in this role — as a powerfully sexually dominant woman. In all her writings, her female characters are strong, bigger than life, owning their sexuality. Their situations are intense and inventive, erotic and hard to look away from. As a Dominatrix, she had ideas.

So many.

This may have been the difference between them.

Where Eve was a creative, innovative sexual top, creating new scenes easily, ideas constantly flowing from her, Jonah was naturally more reserved. His moments of dominance weren't infused with the genius hers were. He loved it.

But she lived it.

Jonah walked, along with the other two men, down the hallway from the kitchen with trays of appetizers. It looked like Marissa did have this entire floor of the building. Investigating, Jonah saw that it was once probably 5 apartments, but since the downturn, had been combined into one big space. He had heard about things like this. Apparently, it was becoming more common that as people left the city, the people around them would buy up the property and merge it, creating larger spaces.

Spaces that often felt empty.

Not this one though, not right now. There might have been about 60 people altogether, at this event. And only three of them, the servers, were men.

And while he and the two other men were entirely naked, the guests were all in various states of dress. Some women were in suits, some in jeans, some exposing some skin, while some were completely naked. Regardless, they all looked comfortable. They looked in charge.

Jonah tried to keep his eyes down as he served, taking drink orders, handing out appetizers, doing what the women wanted. He helped one woman unhook her dress so she could remove it, while going back to the kitchen for a special food request for another.

For the most part they ignored him. They rarely spoke directly to him, choosing instead to snap or wave to make their needs understood. He tried hard to understand what they needed. And he tried not to scratch the part of his skin, on his wrist, that had gotten the third tattoo.

By 9:30 he'd taken three circuits, at least, of the space and still had not seen the pink woman. He thought back about the few seconds in which he'd seen her.

Could she have been wearing some kind of all over bodysuit? Or makeup?

It could have been a full body tattoo.

Or not.

As the evening progressed, more of the women had been touching him. He tried to catalogue it, in his head, to remember to tell Eve everything that had happened. How some woman in the kitchen grabbed his dick while ordering him around, just to get his full attention. Or how Marissa slapped and hit him every time she saw him. Or how her friend with the dark red hair, Arete, kept her hand on his ass while she ordered him around, digging her nails in to make it hurt.

She was the woman who had given him the tattoo. He smelled her unique scent as he turned around. She had stripped down and was wearing only a few chains stretched across her perfect smoothly shaved pussy. He breathed in quickly, against his will.

The second time he saw her was in the hallway as he made his way back for more food. He very nearly bumped into her. He inhaled. She smelled like Lilac, a scent he remembered as he closed his eyes.

She grabbed his arm and pulled him into the bathroom right next to them, hitting him in the side of the head. "Hey, dummy, focus on what you're supposed to be doing."

"Yes, sir."

She moved to the toilet and sat down. He could hear the light splash of her urine hitting the inside of the bowl as she began to pee. "Do you want the rod again?"

Jonah remembered the metal rod inside him. "No, sir."

She finished and leaned back, pushing her cunt out. She flushed the toilet and motioned for him to come over. He moved quickly to her. She was one of the most beautiful women he'd ever seen. She pushed his head down.

"Damn chains."

He began to lick her pussy clean, focusing on the area surrounded by chains, dripping with urine. He pushed his tongue out, trying to widen it, make it flat to catch it all. He inhaled her scent as he licked and he felt his cock engorge. Jonah was terrified that she would see when he got up. He had just started to get lost in it when she pulled his head up and kicked him away. He caught himself before he fell backward.

"Back to work, Jonah."

He started to walk away when she noticed his erection. She stood up and pushed his back against the door, shaking her head. The woman pulled her hand back and slapped his hard cock. He closed his eyes in pain. His cocked bobbed back and forth. He tried to look down, but he could still see her slight smile. She pulled back and slapped it again. He felt the thickness in his dick go down slightly. She hit him over and over again, and each time he felt his prick shrink away, becoming more flaccid, falling to one side. Harder she slapped, catching his balls in her swing. She continued, even when he was completely soft. His dick felt on fire, red and aching. His knees had almost started giving out when she finally stopped.

"I just did you a big favor, Jonah."

He tried to stand up straight, "Thank you, sir."

One of the men was being sodomized in the hallway as he passed by two young dark haired women. They had pushed him up against the wall and one was pushing a large dildo in him while the other was talking to him, taunting him, with her hands roaming all over him. Jonah tried to ignore it as he traversed the corridor on his way to the kitchen. He kept his head down and filled his tray, taking a deep breath as he walked out the other door to deliver the finger snacks to the other room.

And that's when he saw her. The Pink woman

She was completely nude, except for a pair of silver boots, leaning against the wall, with a drink in her hand. She was speaking to a blonde woman and laughing. Jonah tried to get a good look at her as he passed.

It wasn't a suit.

It wasn't makeup

He couldn't place her smell as he passed, but it was musky, raw. If anything, she smelled woody, like teakwood. Jonah remembered when he had first discovered that OUD, his favorite scent, was essentially the smell made by some wood when it rotted.

The smell was powerful. And unique.

She was tall, maybe 4 or 5 inches taller than him, with a bright, expressive face.

He made a show of pretending to drop some napkins from the platter. He stepped over them and turned, bending down to pick them up. This gave him the chance to sneak a peak at her from behind.

And he saw that, from behind, there was a kind of ridge running down her spine, slightly darker, raised. Jonah had no idea what to think. Was this some kind of elaborate advanced stage prosthetics?

Nothing else made any sense.

As he stood up, Marissa was there next to him. She snapped at him to get his attention. "C'mon. In the Library."

He followed her down the hall to the Library. He watched as her ass moved in front of him. She was a pretty girl, dark, vibrant, small but bigger than life. He tried to forget that she was a receptionist. He'd already been so badly humiliated in front of her that she no longer seemed like that person in that office.

She was just another woman he needed to obey. He thought about Eve, about her instructions.

Just do what you're told.

They moved into a large room, clearly converted into a library. In the center of the room was the other naked male server. There were tiny objects sticking out of his skin as he tried to stand up straight.

All around him, women were laughing, talking together, and occasionally tossing these tiny darks at him. Jonah could see they had what looked like hypodermic needles on the front, 28 gauge needles that could be barely felt when they pierced the surface of the skin. Despite that, the other man was trying to protect his cock and balls, causing the women to laugh even harder.

"Stand here for now." Marissa pointed to a nook right by the main Bookshelf. There were a row of books right in his eyesight, lined up in shades from blue to green.

A series.

He tried to blend in and disappear. His eyes ran over the books on the shelf.

And the tabs on the shelves below. One caught his eye immediately. He shifted slightly to his right to get closer. It wasn't possible.

The row of blue-green books each had a large title. "Solara." They appeared to be part of a series. There must have been at least 10 of them. And underneath them was a metal tag, affixed to the wood of the bookshelf. At first, he thought he had read the name wrong. As he looked more closely he saw he had not.

Eve Ungaro.

Had Eve published a book? Had she published a series of books? There was no possible way he could have missed that. He was her biggest supporter, he thought. He had pushed her for years to write a book.

Did she have a bunch of books out?

Marissa snapped, calling him out of his reverie. She pointed to a pillow in the middle of the room. He could see one just like it nearby, where the man who had been the center of the game was lying, face up, while a woman lowered her ass onto his face. They were preparing to watch something.

Getting comfortable.

Marissa grabbed his hand and pushed him down on the pillow. He tried to cross his legs, frog style, as the other man was doing while he readied himself. Marissa faced his legs and slowly lowered her ass onto his face. She was dark and unshaven and her pubic hair was soft and pleasant on his cheeks as his mouth opened to her pussy.

She pressed down, grinding her cunt into his face. Even from his position, Jonah could see the lights begin to dim in the room. Marissa's pussy dripped into his mouth as she pressed it into his face as though he were a toy, a device, something to not think twice about. He felt his face turning red as he experienced this rush of shame. He had worked really hard to get to his position at work. He was a respected project manager, someone who might have been under consideration one day, to run the entire company. He was diligent and kind to the people below him, a good mentor.

None of that mattered. A receptionist could use him, punish him, laugh at him. She could do whatever she wanted to him and no one would care. Grey Shirra-Austen was a powerful woman. She was a boss. She ran an entire government agency with the strength of her will. He had no problem deferring to her.

And Eve was Eve. He adored her. He loved her and fantasized about marrying her. The way they played required that someone be submissive to the other sometimes. They understood. She was so talented, so personally powerful. He didn't feel this in their play.

But here, under this young girl, he felt so ashamed. She'd watched him and laughed at him while he was treated like an animal. And now she shushed him and forced him to be her chair.

She alternated sliding her cunt over his lips and leaning back, forcing her asshole onto his open lips. He licked at her, taking cues from her. She slapped his chest when he was too fast.

She was in control.

He tried to set his shame aside and focus. She tasted thick and salty, sexy, good.

He dug his tongue deeply inside her, trying to get her to flow easily into his mouth. His back felt raw and still abused from Eve the night before, but he put that out of his mind, too.

Occasionally a hand or object played across his cock or ass. At one point, he spread his ass for an object that moved slowly up his asshole. It eventually stopped, holding its position and not moving. A part of him was terrified just not knowing.

Not knowing anything.

The room grew quiet as a woman's voice rang out. She was speaking loudly, reading. She had a slight accent he couldn't place. She read a story called "Yleros Night."

She introduced it as a well known piece of fiction, but Jonah had to admit to himself he'd never heard of it.

It started with a young girl, 17 years old, who grew up unsure, quiet. Her name was Keyo. She wasn't aware of her own power, yet, as so many are not. When her home was destroyed, she cowered in the corner, clinging to the last of her belongings. She shivered, she bled.

She starved.

But when the sun went out, weeks later, she started off on a journey to find it and reignite it.

To reach the mountain where the suns lived, however, she had to travel through strange forests with bizarre creatures that she had to fight and fend off alone. Each one was larger and more ferocious than the last. Jonah had never heard of any of these mythical creatures, but he tried to follow the story as it continued, charting the remarkable sizes and configurations of these beasts, terrifying throwbacks to the ancient ownership of the world by monsters and pre-human creatures.

The woman continued her story.

She told how each night she would return to her thatched cave at the edge of the forest, after having vanquished this beast or that one, ripping their heads from their bodies and taking from each a single pointed tooth. And in her cave, she would clean and shine that tooth until it glistened, mounting it with a metal ring and placing it next to the last, in order of size, on a metal ring.

And every day, the ring grew.

She ate the monsters' hearts and grew strong and fearless. She bathed in their blood and grew harder, thicker, harder to kill. And she squeezed their brains into her water bottle and drank, making her, every day, wiser than the day before.

Then, finally, when she had an entire ring of teeth, she put it around her neck and ascended the mountain to speak to the Twin Sun goddesses. As she approached the peak, the goddess' consort stepped up to stop her. He shone brightly in the borrowed light from his owners. And he was strong.

Keyo reached out with the strength she had earned from each heart and choked him. Her wisdom, gleaned from drinking from their brains, let her know how close he was to death. And her invulnerable skin let her step into Solara's fiery presence unharmed, carrying the body of her consort.

At first, the elder Sun goddess was angry. Who was this mortal woman who killed her pet and broke into her home.

Keyo smiled at her and asked if she was sad about the death of her consort. The elder goddess of the sun said yes, as she loved him in her way, as any might love a man. Keyo then blew breath into him and revived him in front of her, because he wasn't really dead. The Sun Goddess, powerful and mystically enhanced, still did not have the ability to thwart death. She looked at Keyo with a newfound respect and told her she would grant her what she wanted.

All Key wanted was for the Suns themselves to do their job. She warned the Sun goddess that if that were not happening, she would be back.

And 10,000 years passed in the light, because of Keyo.

Jonah was fascinated. It seemed like the kind of myth that might have been invented by some culture to explain sunlight. But it was off. It was strange.

As the story ended, he felt Marissa touch herself, placing her labia directly over his lips. She had been edging on his face for the whole story and now, finally, was ready to let go. He felt her squirting into his mouth, once then twice.

There was so much liquid. It poured down his face, into his hair. She bounced up and down, pressing down on him. Finally, she placed her asshole directly onto his nose, pressed down and pissed a little, just enough to fill his mouth.

He drank it down, just in time as she did it again. She seemed good at peeing in small increments, just enough to fill a man's mouth. He drank, swallowing loudly, as she did it again.

His face felt red and hot. This humiliation didn't seem like something she was doing for fun. Rather it felt like something she did to make sure he felt inferior to her. He had no choice but to defer to her. He could no longer think of her as some young receptionist. She was part of something he didn't understand.

This was bigger.

He put his clothes on in the outer room as Marissa entered, again in her robe. He let his eyes fall downward. He wanted to find answers, but he knew she wouldn't give him any.

She lifted his head. "Starting next week, I'm going to work for you." She lifted his wrist to show the pips. "You have two months to get 10 of these and then we'll tell you anything you want to know, ok?"

He nodded. It was better than he had hoped.

Marisa forced him to make eye contact. "Do you understand? This is your ring of teeth."

Jonah responded, "Yes, sir."

She started to walk away. Then she turned. "Jonah. You did good tonight. The next time, you bring another helper, right?"

Jonah nodded and breathed out as she exited the room.

Chapter 7

Jonah slid into bed with Eve when he got home. All he wanted was her smell, the taste of her, the way she felt. He put his hand between the cheeks of her ass, as if for warmth, while he wrapped the other around her chest, pulling her close. She always felt perfect against him.

He kissed her ear.

She responded groggily, "How was that?"

He laughed a little, "That was intense. And surreal."

She turned into him. "Do you want to fuck me before you crash?"

He could feel how comfortable she was. She was wearing her tiny white velour shorts. Usually, when she wanted to be fucked before bedtime, she'd be bottomless.

"How about we take a half day and make the morning our bitch." He licked her ear.

"I like it. I'm in." She dug into him deeper and they drifted off to sleep.

Jonah dreamt about the story he had heard. It was interesting, but somehow off. Most cultures considered the earth the mother and the sun the father. What cultures had a sun goddess? He thought the Japanese did but she didn't have a consort. That wasn't a common idea, either, women having a consort. The Keyo character was also female.

It didn't seem traditional, but it also didn't seem modern. In his dream, he was in the cave with her, helping her. He helped her bleach the teeth, mount them. He bathed her and took care of her.

He fretted when she went off to fight. And rejoiced with her when she came home, making her food.

He wasn't a main character. He didn't even have a name. But he was there. He helped. In his mind, she was Eve. Eve was the main character.

So, what was he?

***

Eve was in the kitchen when he got up, in a pair of white socks and a white tank top that did a terrible job of covering any of her. Jonah particularly loved this outfit, not just because it was brilliant to look at but also because Eve was so often wet that eventually every part of him would be covered with her pussy juice.

Before Jonah, she had dated a guy from Princeton who discouraged her from being bottomless. He kept telling her it was a hygiene issue. He would even put towels down when she didn't remember. For the first year she and Jonah were together, she had been insecure about it, even hiding her constantly wet panties in the depths of the hamper. It took Jonah a while to convince her that he didn't want anything around that didn't smell like her or taste like her. One of his favorite things was her sitting on his leg kissing him as he felt the wetness sink into his clothing. He would daydream at work, touching the spot, Trying to smell her.

And when she walked around like this, he could just slip his fingers in her casually as they talked, enjoying the silky wet warmth of her inner spaces.

Jonah wanted to be that free. He walked up to her as she cooked and kissed her. As if reading his mind, she turned and pulled his boxers down, letting his cock swing free. He bent over and grabbed them, tossing them in the open bedroom door.

She laughed, "There you go."

Jonah hugged her. "It's not as cool as when you do it."

"Bullshit. Breakfast is almost done."

He shook his head, "I could have…"

"Nope. You served last night."

Jonah winced in embarrassment thinking about last night. "I sure did."

Eve filled a plate for him with eggs and sausage. "Are you going to tell me all about it?" She smiled and sat down next to him, one knee up. He tried not to look at her between the legs and failed badly. By the time he looked up, she was smiling at him. She reached in her pussy and pulled her hand out sopping wet, slipping it into his mouth.

This was breakfast.

He closed his eyes. "Thank you."

"Was it fun at all?" She seemed really excited to know. Jonah realized that her excitement was wrapped around his journey of submission. He was so over the top about him being a slave.

"You want me to say yes, don't know?"

"If that's true. Do you like it?"

Jonah took a breath. Her enthusiastic interest was making him hard. Eve slid her hand over his cock and started massaging it. "I do. I like superior women. Like you."

"You think I'm superior?"

"I don't think anyone is worthy of you, certainly not me. I think you are a hero. I'm just here to serve you."

She reached under her top and pulled the key out, fondling it. Jonah leaned forward and licked it.

She smiled. "Fuck. you are so fucking hot."

Jonah was afraid to ask this next question. He didn't want to ruin the mood. Her hands both massaged him between the legs now, one holding his balls.

"What is Solara?"

She stopped for a second and then smiled and continued. "A series of books that you will love one day."

"Did you write a book already? Some books?"

"They're not ready."

"Oh my god, Eve, I want to read them."

Eve looked around, "Eggs are good cold, right?" She pulled him into the bedroom. Pushing him onto the bed, she put her fingers inside herself again and rubbed them all over his face. He laughed.

"That's extra. That's because I get too wet around you." She climbed on him and lifted his cock, impaling herself on it.

He breathed in and moaned. "Extra, huh?"

"I have so much extra around you. Is it okay that I'm a drippy fountain?"

Hearing her say that almost made Jonah cum. References to Eve's body fluids didn't give him much chance. And she knew it.

"Can you feel how sloppy?" She kissed him wetly on the mouth.

"I love it so much."

"I feel wet and sweaty and messy. I need a shower." She taunted him.

Jonah tried not to cum immediately. "No you don't, baby. You know I want to eat you first."

"Before my shower? After all this exertion?"

Jonah laughed, "Oh fuck you. I'm going to cum anyway."

She pressed his cheeks together. "Oh, no, I think I squirted on you. I better clean that up. And be careful, my ass is all sweaty."

Jonah stopped breathing as he tried to hold back.

"I should have asked you to lick my sweaty ass, baby." She smiled down at him. Eve loved how just talking about her wetness, sweat, anything, could drive him stupid crazy.

Jonah made noises and kept pumping his cock into her.

"Ohhhh. I'm going to squirt again." She grabbed her breasts and grinded on his dick. "I hope you can clean up the mess with your pretty mouth.

Jonah was breathing hard. He could barely think. She leaned in

"Am I your favorite drink? Am I your smoothie, my pussy juice? Do you want it to suck on? Do you want to drink it all, baby? Can you hear how messy it is?

The thing is, he could. Every time they slapped together with his prick digging into her, he could hear the wet splash of her, leaking all over him. The sound of Eve never being dry, never being cold or uninterested.

Just being alive.

He let out a moan and came in her. "I'm cumming, I'm cumming."

She wrapped her arms around his head and pressed her tits into him. Her shirt was wet and sweaty and she was all over him. She leaned in and he opened her mouth. She spit in it and Jonah swallowed.

Eve slid down him, kissing his chest and nipples. She put her tongue in his bellybutton and followed his belly down, wrapping her mouth around his sopping wet dick. She rubbed her hands against his wet balls and into the sloppy mess she had made all over him. She could feel the lubrication all over his ass and balls as she let her right hand slide down and dip into his ass pulling him up so she could bury her face in his dick.

Her fingers slid deeper into him while she tried to grab a roll of flesh around his tummy, using both as handles to eat his prick, sucking and licking it as she fucked her own face with his midsection. Jonah felt out of control and unable to do anything but let go and become limp, while she gnawed at his root like an animal, trying as hard as she could to swallow his balls along with his half-tumescent cock. At first, he wasn't sure if he could come again, but then, as she kept going, he stopped caring. It didn't matter if he was getting hard or if he could cum, he just needed to let go and let her chew and suck on him like some kind of demon animal, violating his ass with one hand and forcing him into her mouth like he was meat at a zoo.

She climbed over him, sticking her ass in the air. He could smell her sweat and it made him try to dig his face into her underarms. He couldn't reach, but this seemed to make her even more animal-like. She lifted him with one hand cupped in his asshole, smashing his body into her face as though she was drinking the last few drops from a bottle. He went limp, spreading his ass even more so she could dig her hand in it, feeling her knuckles wrench their way past his sphincter. He felt so dirty and wet and covered in her body fluids, slippery and raw. Her fist closed inside his rectum and it felt impossibly big. She punched at him from the inside, waking up his prostate, forcing him to spring erect in her sopping wet mouth. She climbed up him, sticking her foot in his mouth as she dug her knee into his chest trying to own the prick in her mouth and bleed it dry.

He heard her growl like a wolf as she tried to claim a foothold in his mouth with her bare foot. Her sock had fallen off and Jonah tried his best to suck her toes into his throat, letting her violate his open mouth with her dirty feet. he felt it bang up in the back of his throat, threatening to slide down his gullet, and he tried to swallow, making his throat wet enough to be fucked by her pretty toes, scrathing the back of his throat raw. Her fingers wrapped around his prostate and he felt the cum pour out of him in waves, almost as if it was coming from deep inside him. She drank him and bit down on the base of his cock, making him scream.

When he came all he could, Eve picked him up and threw him forcibly against the wall behind the bed.

He hit with a satisfying thud and scrambled to a crouching position watching her do the same. Her eyes were feral, animalistic. She was breathing hard and covered in both of their body fluids. He moved forward, feeling like a chimpanzee, and pushed his face into her underarms. She pulled him in, rubbing his face in her, pushing him down and suffocating him in her. He tried to pet her calmly but it seemed to send her into an unthinking frenzy. She pulled off her top and jumped on top of him, shoving her right breast into his face as though she meant to nurse him. He clamped on and suckled her. For a moment, he almost felt like there was milk coming out, merging with the hot wet mess they had both become.

She grabbed a fistfull of his hair and sat down hard on his face, rubbing the sweat of her ass into the skin on his face. He licked and sucked on her with abandon, trying to clean her as well as he could. His tongue, gently lapping at the tiny hole between her cheeks seemed to soothe her. She rocked back and forth, holding him and placing little kisses all over his skin.

They ate breakfast in bed and talked about what had been done to Jonah the night before. She was excited to hear it all. It was clear when he talked about certain things that she knew more than he did. For some reason she didn't feel comfortable telling him. So he didn't push it.

"So you like superior women?"

"Well, I have always liked strong women. Can I be honest with you?"

Eve laughed, taking a bite of toast. "Of course."

"It's easy for me to think of you as superior. And Grey, I mean, she is obviously superior, too. I mean, that is a no brainer. But there is a part of me that has so much trouble thinking of someone like Marissa as superior to me."

"How come?"

"I mean, I don't want to be an asshole. But she's young. She's just this tiny thing. She's a receptionist. I looked at her file at work. She didn't graduate high school. She has a GED.

Is it wrong that it's really hard for me to see it?"

"Does a woman HAVE to be superior in certain ways for you to respect her?"

"No, of course not. I mean, I can respect her all day. But submission to her? I mean, you should see what she was doing to me."

"I know. I heard. She's cute, though?"

"Yes, she's very pretty. But she's insulting me and degrading me and punishing me, pissing on me, forcing me to serve her..."

"And it wasn't hot?"

"I guess it was. It's just. A lot to wrap my head around."

"Let me ask you a question." She put the plate down and set herself right in front of Jonah.

"Ok." He looked into her eyes. She was clearly very intense right now.

"What if this was the world? What if EVERY woman had to be treated like they were superior to you? What if the last couple of weeks or so was how it always was?"

"Where I do what women tell me to?"

"Yes. All the time. Outside. In your life. You obey women."

"I don't know."

"It would be sexy and fun and you would have fewer responsibilities. You would be taken care of."

"Taken care of?"

"Loved. Cherished."

"Well. it doesn't sound terrible like that."

Eve smiled. "In private, you could do anything you wanted to me.

You could use me, order me around, beat me. But no one could know."

"No one could know, huh? I don't think I broadcast that now."

She laughed. "Like when you kicked my cunt and broke it because you only needed my ass that night." She crawled in and kissed his neck.

"I liked that."

"You could do anything in private."

"I don't know. I'd have to think about it."

She leaned back against the bedpost. "Do you want to get two pips tonight?"

Jonah looked at her. He wished he could know everything that she knew. "What happens when I have 10?"

Eve looked confused for a minute. "What do you mean?"

He sighed. "Nevermind." He took a deep breath. "Yes, I do want to get two." He had earned one pip for last night. At this point, he couldn't imagine what he would have to do to get two. He almost asked her, but Eve's secrets were hers.

They got ready to leave. He texted Giselle:

A naked picture for my partner.

And waited. It took less than a minute for her to send a shot through. It looked as though it might have been in a doctor or Nurse's lounge. She had pulled her clothes off and they lay crumpled at her feet. Her hands were at her side. It looked obedient. He wondered if he would ever be that obedient.

He texted back:

I'll get you at your place tomorrow

There were dots as she wrote her response:

Yes, Sir

He showed the picture to Eve who thought she was lovely. "What do YOU think of her?"

Jonah thought for a second. "She's kind of fascinating. She's really obedient and fun."

Eve put her hand in his. "Do you like that?"

Jonah felt the secure squeeze of her hand. Was it ok to say he didn't know?

"I think I'm learning what I like."

She laughed as they stepped out of the apartment. "That's fair. Do you want to know what we're doing tonight?"

"I assume I'm serving. Twice as hard as last night."

"Well. not exactly. Honestly, you are my guest tonight. You are my partner tonight."

"Oh, really?" Jonah considered what that might mean, given the situations they'd been in.

"You do have to do what I say. But you'll have a pass. You'll get to speak to us."

"Us?" Jonah asked, "Who else is going?"

"Oh, I thought I told you. Grey is coming with us. You like her, right?"

Jonah thought about the last time he'd seen Grey and how she'd treated him like a cow, like a piece of livestock. He couldn't imagine just hanging out with her, spending time with her.

"I do. I think."

"Do you trust me?" Eve kissed him lightly. He closed his eyes and drank her in.

"I trust you too much."

She slapped him on the ass. "Good. That's how it should be. Let's get fucked up tonight."

He laughed, "Yeah, that's what we're doing?"

She swung her bag and made her way to the car, laughing.

And Jonah climbed into his. He tried to imagine what he would have to do for two pips.

Nothing came to him.

Chapter 8

Marissa was in Jonah's office when he got in. Keith was already there, huddled behind his laptop on the couch.

Jonah sat down behind his desk. "I didn't realize you were starting today."

"I figured I may as well. I'm keeping my other office for... privacy, but I'll work out there in the bullpen."

Keith looked up, "You can work in here with us."

Marissa cocked her head at Jonah.

"Oh, he knows." he said.

She smiled, "oh. Bring him next time."

Keith raised his hand. "I'm a trans man."

Marissa nodded at Jonah. "A man."

He followed up, "And I don't know how kinky I am."

She laughed. "He'll learn."

Keith raised his hand. "Sitting right here."

Jonah stepped around and sat on his desk. "I mean, you are welcome to work here. But how does all this work?"

She crossed her legs. "How about this? In this office, your office, I'm your secretary. You can even hit on me. Slap me on the ass. Hard. I like it. Don't let HR know." she pointed a pencil at him.

Keith shook his head, "So, NOW, there's an HR?"

"Everywhere else, I'm superior to you and you answer to me."

Jonah grunted a little involuntarily. He looked at Keith. "Do you hear this?"

"I think you SHOULD slap that ass."

"Can you help me manage my schedule? I mean, if I'm going to get ten of these..." he lifted his hand."

"Yep. I will run your personal schedule, too."

He squinted at her. She was businesslike, yes, but so different from last night. "Are you coming to this thing tonight?"

Keith perked up. "There's a thing?"

Jonah nodded. Marissa looked at her book in front of her. "I am not. And you are at Archon tomorrow night with Giselle and Eve, too."

She stood up to leave. Jonah asked, "And when is your next event?"

She turned to him. "It's next week. It's already on your calendar. And you have a general meeting with me at three in my office today."

"In your office?"

"Yes. You've been there. Until then I'll be right there or here. Let me know if you need anything."

"Sounds great." Jonah sat back down as she left.

Keith slowly closed his computer. "Can I speak here?"

"I don't know if that's a good idea."

"Are you planning to do any work here anymore or is this just a sex shop?"

"Hey. I was putting all the sprints together while you were fucking off."

"Ok, fair, but I'm good at fucking off.

Jonah looked out into the Bullpen. "Where did everyone go?"

"I don't know, man. Every day, people are just... you know... Gone. They go work at home, They move away. They retire early. They get out. The work is drying up. All of it is bullshit.

Jonah sighed, "This place is a ghostland."

"It is. I mean, I'm still here. Forced to share your office because they got me sitting next to Louis."

"So, you aren't kinky at all?"

Keith thought for a second. "You know. Gender isn't a fun game to me. I fought to be this gender. So any kink that plays off that, I can't do. I don't love pain. I don't like to tell people what to do. So..."

"What do you think about me being told what to do by some 20 something 5 foot girl?"

"I don't know, man. She's cute. I mean, I'd do something with her. I just haven't thought that far ahead." Keith left his computer on the couch as he got up. "Look, man. Settle in. I'm going to get a couple tacos for you and then we'll dive in. Gotta keep your strength up."

"ha ha"

Jonah had some tacos and got some work done. This meeting at three was hanging over his head. Had he misbehaved somehow?

He looked at the clock seemingly every 20 minutes until it was time. He closed up his laptop and made his way to the other wing. It was darker than even before. Jonah realized there were no windows here. He walked down the corridor and knocked on the door.

"Open."

He opened the door and stepped in. It was dark, but there must have been about 40 flickering candles all over the room. It took him a second for his eyes to adjust to the light. And then he saw Marissa. She was in her black fuzzy robe, open in the front. She seemed different - less martial and businesslike. She walked up to him and kissed him softly on the lips, wrapping her arms around him. He kissed her back. Her lips were cushiony and wet, velvety. He opened his mouth and pulled him in, her tongue wrapping around his.

"I'm afraid to talk." Jonah smiled at her.

"I know." She dropped her robe.

"You did just confuse the hell out of me." He leaned back in and kissed her again.

She gently put his hands on her breasts. "Eve said you were having some trouble seeing me as superior."

"Oh, she did? Does she tell you everything we talk about?"

She kissed his neck and started unbuttoning his shirt "She could. She owns you, right?"

Jonah had never thought of that. Is that what was happening?

Marissa pulled his shirt off and started moving them to the corner. She kissed him again.

Jonah saw a large bed, with black sheets and pillows in the corner. It wasn't there the last time he was here, was it? Marissa slid back onto the bed, nude, and spread her legs, pulling him in between them. She unbuttoned his pants and pulled them down.

"You know. Some people, you can tell right away they're superior. Like Eve. And Grey. You can't avoid it. You submit to them because they are powerful. And they are better than you."

He nodded. He let her disrobe him completely. Her voice sounded wonderful in the flickering dark.

She continued. "Some people, though. You have to really like them. And then that's the lens you can see them through. To see their power."

Jonah nodded "Ah. And you want me to like you?"

"You *will* like me."

"Eve's idea?"

Marissa smiled and nodded kindly. Her hand moved up and down on his cock as she leaned back. He looked down. The hair under her arms and over her pussy was dark black and so soft looking. Her skin was dark and seamless, smooth all over. Her breasts were full and large, but new looking, as though they had just been made. Leaning back as she was, there was a tiny little crease in her tummy, right above her belly button. A tiny roll that he wanted to run his tongue over.

The truth is that it had taken her just a few minutes to make him like her. Was he this easy? He reached down between her legs and felt a welcoming warm wetness. He remembered the feel of her lips on his face last night and breathed in, imagining the pretty smell. She let out a tiny moan as his finger slipped in her, exploring her.

He lifted his finger to his mouth.

There it was.

What he had tasted last night. Suddenly, she felt familiar. His body recognized her.

It was Marissa.

He crawled forward and slid himself into her open pussy as she spread her legs wider and moaned.

"Can you stay there?"

He nodded.

"You should be right there all the time. How does it feel in me?"

"It's so good."

She smiled and touched his face. "You have a nice curve. There's a spot that never usually gets touched."

He pushed in another inch. She moaned.

"That. that one there. Nothing ever touches that."

He bent down and kissed her slowly. He could feel her languidly roll her hips back and forth.

"I like how you're pressing into me. I feel the base of your cock on me."

He pressed again, trying to match her back and forth movement.

"This is how I masturbate sometimes. I put something in me and just move my clit back and forth."

"Like this?" he moved slowly again.

She laughed. "Just like that. It's better when you do it."

She moved like a belly dancer under him. Her motions were slow and erotic and kind. This was a completely different woman.

But it wasn't.

He pushed himself in again and she touched her clit. "Now, when I say, pull out for a second."

She kept moving slowly, but her fingers increased in speed, moving back and forth. "Now."

Jonah quickly pulled out and watched her pretty belly buckle and shake. The little rolls became more pronounced and her breasts shook while a stream of liquid poured out of her. She kept manipulating her clit as the water sprayed through her fingers. Jonah slid down to try to catch it in his mouth. She shook, making the bed quake a little. She stopped, breathing hard, her hand between her legs. About a minute later, she pulled him back up to kiss him.

"Did you get any?"

Jonah laughed. "I did. I wish it were more."

She kissed him deeply. Slipping his cock back in her. "You know it's that curve you have."

"You taste good. Can you do it again? I'll be more ready."

They slowly began moving back and forth again. Jonah pressed in, listening for her moans. He was starting to feel like he understood how her pussy worked.

That was an amazing feeling.

He felt her fingers smashed between the two of them, as they moved more intensely and this time she didn't have to tell him when.

He slid out and quickly moved his face between her legs, licking, sucking and swallowing her. Her breathing slowed and she relaxed. In the candle light, he could see the wetness in her hair and he leaned up to suck it. She played with his hair and giggled.

He slid up and kissed her on the lips. "What's so funny?"

She pulled him back on top of her. "You know what sucks about that Twillerex stuff?"

Jonah smiled and shook his head.

She pushed his prick back into her. Her pussy felt incredibly open and wanting. "If I beg you to breed me, you won't believe it."

"Sure I will. Try it."

She smiled as he started pumping into her. "Fuck. Jonah Fucking breed me. Cum in me. Put a baby in my fucking cunt, please." She looked up and caressed his face. "Please Please."

"You want me to fill you up, baby?"

She whined, "Yes, please. Just breed me. Make me your cumdump. I want it all. I don't care. Please"

Jonah caressed her face. "Look how pretty you are. I would love to knock you up. Can you lift your legs?"

She lifted her legs and wrapped them around his waist, nodding frantically. "Yes, yes, please, just give me all your cum. I want you to breed me."

She dropped her arms to her side, the way people do when they want to be open, to be used, to offer no resistance. She pulled Jonah in with her legs

"He petted her hair. "You're doing so good. Now keep that hole open for me, ok?"

She nodded over and over again, "yes, yes, yes."

Now as soon as you cum, I'll breed you ,baby, I'll pour all my cum in you."

Her eyes looked so plaintive. This Marissa was so beautiful. And she submitted so perfectly, with the one thing she wanted right now. Jonah loved that he could give it to her.

"I'm cumming" She called out. Jonah felt the small splash between her legs as it flowed out of her. It triggered something in him. He felt the warmth, the building power of his own orgasm.

"Good, baby. Now I'm going to cum in you. Open your cunt baby. I want to cum right into your cervix. " She lifted her legs higher and he pounded straight up and down until he came, so hard, inside her. He let out a muted yell and exploded. She wrapped her arms around him and hugged him tightly.

They breathed together for about 5 minutes just holding each other. He ran his hand over her hair. She licked at his lips.

"I know you have to get back to work. Do you want to fuck my ass before you go?"

Jonah sighed. I'm not sure I have it in me.

She whispered, "Next time?"

Jonah kissed her. "Is there going to be a next time?"

She kissed him back. "There'll be lots of different times. I'd like to fuck YOUR ass. If that's ok?"

"You want me on my stomach or back?" Jonah asked between kisses. This was closer to what he thought would happen when he came here. But she was asking him. Not telling him. That was something.

"Well, I'd like to see your pretty face." She kneeled, caressing his face.

Jonah laughed, "Pretty, huh?"

Can I tell you a secret?

This was curious. Jonah nodded.

"Tonight. You're being filmed. They want to see that you can respect women enough to let yourself be like one."

"Who wants to? Grey?"

"Yes. And more. It's going to feel weird. You love women."

He nodded. "I do."

"Can you be a woman for me right now?"

"You mean, while you fuck me?"

Marissa nodded. She moved to her desk and pulled out a strap on. It was larger than Jonah's cock, but not overly large. She slid it into a harness and pulled it up.

"You want me to be your girlfriend?"

She nodded. "You aren't afraid of being a woman?"

Jonah smiled and shook his head. "Most of my close friends are women. Hell, my best friend was born a woman. Don't say that to him."

She kissed him again and pulled him to the bed. He laid down on his back and lifted his legs, wrapping his arms around them.

She climbed onto him and moved up his body, aiming the dildo at his face. He stretched his neck out and tried to pull it down his throat.

"Make your mouth as wet as you can. " Marissa tried to guide him.

Jonah nodded.

She slowly sunk the dildo between his lips, lodging it into his throat. She swallowed over and over, trying to pull it into the back of his throat, while his hands caressed her ass, pulling as hard as he could.

She pressed down on his legs and rode his face. He gagged but pulled her in even deeper. He imagined Marissa could feel it and he tried to do his best.

He didn't realize how deep it had gone until she pulled it loose and he heard a little pop in the back of his throat

She slid down his body and positioned the black silicone prick at the opening of his ass. Marissa kissed him and caressed his face. "Are you ready?"

Jonah tried to feel as feminine as possible. "I want you so bad."

She started pushing it into him. "You want this?"

"Please, baby? I want your cock so bad." He lifted his ass another two inches so she slid in easily. "Oh, yes. Marissa. You're so fucking good. Please fuck me."

Marissa laughed. "I got you, baby. Just spread your legs. Open up for me."

"Yes, yes. I will, just don't stop. Please give me your beautiful cock." Jonah imagined all the things he loved being told. Everything that worked for him.

"Do you want to be my pretty girl?" Marissa started moving rhythmically back and forth like a piston.

"I do, baby. I want you to love me and fill me up." Jonah tried to match her exact rhythm

Marissa whispered to him, "This is what you do tonight, ok, Jonah?"

"Yes, I will. I wish you could feel me up and breed me. I wish you could use me all the time."

"There's no shame in being penetrated, is there?" Marissa whispered conspiratorially.

"No, my holes want you so bad. Fuck me as hard as you want." Jonah felt himself getting lost in this part. Later, he would try to parse his feelings for Marissa. But for now, she was his secret teller, his womb, his man.

"Marissa, please screw me, fuck me, use me. I want your cock so bad. Breed me."

"It's ok, baby. Just keep open. I'm going to pump into you hard, okay, like I like. Can you handle it?"

Jonah nodded, "Please, destroy my asshole, just do what you want. I want your hot cum in me. Please."

Marissa was breathing hard. She pushed his legs back even harder, lifting herself up and pumped the rod into him over and over. Her thighs were swimming in pain but she kept at it. She counted strokes until finally found herself at 100. She cried out and slammed into him three more times.

"Fuck yes." Jonah's arms and legs fell flat on the bed. He was covered in sweat.

Marissa leaned back on her ass and pulled the strap on off, throwing it toward the desk. She climbed up Jonah's body and kissed him.

"Are you ok?" She held his face in her hands.

He was breathing hard. It took him a second to respond. "I'm ok, Marissa. I'm good. That was tough. But it was good."

"You did great." She licked at his lips. He had come to like it when she did that.

"You're still going to be mean to me at your next party." He kissed her.

She slowly kissed him back and nodded. "So mean."

He laughed. "Ok, fine, bring it on."

She put her hands on his cock in a way that felt friendly, comforting. "But will you fuck my ass afterward, just like that?"

"Just like that, huh?"

She squeezed. "Exactly like that."

They made out for a while and then he got up to leave. He turned to her. "I'll see you back at the office."

And that's when Marissa blew him a kiss.

Chapter 9

Jonah had texted Giselle instructions to spend time that night stretching out her pussy, in preparation for tomorrow. So she had been sending him a string of images with objects buried deep inside her. She was definitely putting in the work. And she seemed to enjoy it. Some of the shots also included objects in her ass and one showed novelty baseball bats in all three of her holes. Many of the images involved vegetables, leading Jonah to wonder if she might have been a vegetarian.

He drove to the address that Eve had sent and waited in the car. He found parking right in front of the building, one with a sign in front that read "The Sylo" with a lower case y, just as it was on the sign for "Yleros."

He waited about 5 minutes until he saw Grey and Eve together stepping toward the building. He opened the car door and walked toward them. Eve's face lit up when she saw him. She ran up and wrapped her arms around him, kissing him. "You worked things out with Marissa."

It was a statement, not a question. He nodded. He was getting used to the idea that everyone knew everything and he was in the dark.

They made their way to the door and through the first foyer. Eve pulled out her key and opened the inner door.

This space was brighter than the other clubs. It had the atmosphere of a classy restaurant. But still, she could see, to one side, the table where a large woman stood next to a list of rules identical to Yleros. Eve looked at him and he stepped over, removing his clothes. The woman behind the table motioned to him to remove them all.

He stripped, folding his clothing and placing it on the table. The woman behind it was one of the tallest women he'd ever seen. She was wearing a smart black suit that barely contained her muscles. She reached over and dragged Jonah up on the table, casually putting her thumb in his rectum to cup his ass and hold him down, just as Gerald had done with Giselle.

Jonah's face burnt red in shame while she pushed him down with an elbow and tattooed two tiny circles on his wrist.

Now there were 5.

She put the gun down and started feeling his testicles. She pulled at his cock, leaving him slightly hard before grabbing a hypodermic and injecting him right above in, in the pubic area.

His dick went instantly limp. She let go of him, pushing him off the table. She handed him a piece of fabric.

Eve sidled up next to him. "Put that on. It's just a sundress. It's light."

He pulled it on. It barely covered him. "What was that injection?"

"It prevents you from getting hard for 12 hours." she whispered.

A feeling of panic washed over him. What kind of medication was that? He didn't think anything like that was possible.

The two women pulled off their coats. They were wearing little black dresses as well. He could see a flash of pussy as Grey removed her coat. They were both naked underneath. He slid next to Eve and she pulled him closer.

She whispered in his ear. "I figured that this would be a good place to talk."

They stepped into the main area of the Sylo. It looked much like a traditional bar. The servers moved around, carrying trays of drinks. They were all men, completely naked except for shoes and kneepads.

Every one of them was erect.

Grey looked at him and smiled. "You received a shot that makes it so you can't get hard. These men, serving, can't get soft. "

Jonah thought for a second. "Is that safe?"

"Yes. It's perfectly safe." She snapped for a server and a tall light skinned man with blonde hair walked over. She pulled him closer and turned him around. "This device, on his back, is connected to a metal rod that is inserted into his anus. It connects to his prostate. The medication inflates semen production and the device, called an Elyx, can trigger an ejaculation with the push of a button. It hurts to wear, but fucking feels good. And cumming feels great." She pressed a button on the device and he began shaking, cum shot out of him onto the floor as he moaned.

Jonah remembered the party. He thought he'd experienced that. He looked around. The men all seemed handsome and well endowed. He wondered if he would have cut it as a server.

Grey let go of the server and they moved over to a table. She snapped and pointed to the table. Three men put down trays and walked quickly over to the table. They each lifted the tops from the benches arrayed around the table and laid down in the groove inside, their cocks sticking out from holes in the benches. You could barely see the men anymore, their faces obscured by the top of the bench. Grey put one leg over the table and sat down, impaling herself on the prick sticking out from the hole on the bench.

On their own side of the table, Eve put her leg over and lowered herself onto the man's dick. Jonah got a flash of her pussy and it looked sopping wet as it sunk onto the thick rod. Eve motioned for Jonah to sit.

He looked at the shaft sticking out from the hole. It was large. The man was tall, black, muscular. Jonah put one foot over and positioned himself over the prick, pushing down, sinking onto it. Finally he was seated, listening to Eve and Grey talk.

Grey was sitting still, but Eve was rocking back and forth with a wide smile on her face. She reached over to hold Jonah's hand "You have permission to talk at the table here."

He felt the man in the bench slowly start to fuck him through the hole. He tried to concentrate on the conversation. Eve was moving in such a sexy, feminine way. Remembering Marissa's warning, he tried to channel his feminine side by slowly rocking.

Eve Giggled. "That's it. Let him fuck you. You like that?"

Jonah nodded. He relaxed his ass and tried to emulate her slinkiness. "It's good."

Grey spoke up. "If there is anything you want to try, Jonah, all these men are at our disposal. And there is this." She reached over to a small button in front of Eve that Jonah hadn't seen. She pressed it. Suddenly Eve shot up straight as the man under her pumped his cum into her wet open cunt. She closed her eyes and rubbed her breasts.

Jonah saw the button in front of everyone. Many of the other women all across the club seemed to have one of the men in them.

"As Eve said, this seemed like a good place to talk."

Jonah nodded. He was trying to focus. Grey reached over and pushed the button in front of him and the prick inside him began to pump and push, fucking him harder as it spreyed hot wet cum deep into him. He put his hands on the bench to steady himself.

Jonah was still relatively new to all of this. This was only the second cock he had ever had inside him. A man came over to take their drink orders. Eve grabbed his dick and played with it as she told him to bring them lemonades with a shot of vodka each. She kissed the head of his cock before he left.

Grey laughed, "You like that one."

Eve smiled. "I do. I'm going to have that in my asshole tonight."

It was powerfully hot hearing Eve talk like this, but Jonah's cock was still floppy between his legs. He felt deeply rejected that he couldn't do these things for her. He tried to lean in to the feeling of enjoying her getting what she wanted.

Grey shot him a half smile. "Right now, you're thinking what if this shot ends up being permanent. It won't be." She opened a menu

He nodded.

She continued. "And you're wondering if you are good looking and have a good enough dick to be a server here. And yes. If you need an extra pip at some point, you can do a night here. It's brutal." She reached over and pressed the button in front of her, moving slightly as she was filled from the prick under her.

He nodded. She did seem to understand.

"Eve loves you, you know. Even if she seems preoccupied right now." She pressed Eve's button again and Jonah could hear her squeal as she fucked the man below her. She played with her clit and leaned over the table. He looked at her wistfully.

Grey continued. "Jonah, what if I told you that the world wasn't what you thought it was?"

"I think we all have a feeling somehow that's true"

"How much of that do you believe?"

Jonah was feeling strange. He was trying to play along with Eve and Grey. He squeezed Eve's hand and kissed her. Pushing the button in front of him. She laughed and stuck her tongue in his mouth. She was really letting go here and she seemed to love the idea that he might be having fun. He looked at Grey.

"Test me. Tell me what's going on."

Grey sighed. She rolled her head around and closed her eyes. Jonah playfully pressed the button in front of her and she shot him a glare that quickly turned into a perverse smile. She grabbed his hand. Eve stood up. She was dripping all over. She called over a server who brought a towel, wiping her down and claning off the cock below her. She motioned for Jonah to stand up.

"We're switching." She took a step over to his seat and helped lift him off the bench. She kissed him with a wide, wet, open mouth and grabbed his ass. Jonah put his hands on her inner thighs and felt how wet they were. The server had cleaned the man's cock that had been inside him and he watched now as she slowly lowered her ass onto him, pulling her cheeks apart so it could invade her pretty smaller hole.

Jonah looked down at the prick that was inside her. He pushed his ass down onto it, thinking that it was just fucking Eve. It was smaller but the fact that it had just come from Eve made him hot. It was so warm from being inside her.

Grey called over the server from earlier. He walked over quickly.

"Yes, sir."

She waved at him, lost in the cock inside her for a second. "Shut the fuck up. One second."

Eve laughed and hit the button in front of her. Jonah saw her face as the man's hot cum shot up her ass.

Grey pulled the server in. "Go upstairs with her."

"Yes, sir."

Eve gave Jonah a kiss and stood up, grabbing the server's hand. He watched her disappear up the stairs with him. When he turned back to Grey she had stood up. "Come into the garden with me."

They walked out a large set of glass doors into an interior garden. She held his hand and moved him to a pretty grotto with a small waterfall behind them. It fell into a natural looking pond. Grey pulled her dress off and slid down, sitting on the edge with her legs spread. She motioned to him to get in.

He pulled the dress off and dipped into the water. It was deep. Even though the pool was only about 10 feet wide, it was nearly 5 feet deep. He stood by her and she pulled his face between her legs. "Clean me out."

Jonah licked at her. She was filled with so much cum it was hard to taste what was actually her. He sucked her lips and dug the cum from her pussy and ass with his tongue. Her cunt was beautiful and he knew without the medication he would have been hard as the rocks around them. He tried not to think of the server upstairs who was most likely fucking Eve's ass by now. He loved the way her ass felt when he, himself, fucked it.

Grey ran her fingers over his hair. "I know you're not thinking about me. But focus."

He redoubled his efforts, sucking mouthfuls of cum from her cunt. She flipped over and spread her legs, letting him access her ass better, licking and sucking the cum from there as well. She slid down into the water and turned, kissing him.

"Hmm. you taste good now."

Jonah knew his face was covered in cum. He wanted to go underwater, but she was holding onto his flaccid dick and balls with a serious grip. She seemed to enjoy the fact that he couldn't get hard, and holding on to him this way made sure he couldn't forget it.

Grey looked at him and whispered. "What if I said this planet is only 20,000 years old?"

Jonah looked at her confused. "Do you think that's something you're likely to say?"

"Smart. I like you." She pulled him into the center of the pool and dunked his head.

He came up, feeling cleaner.

"20,134 years old."

"Wait, you're serious." Jonathan tried to scan her face. Was she serious.

"Is this a religious thing?"

"No, Jonah this is a science thing. I've discovered that there is a right order to tell people these things. An order that is most comfortable. That's the first piece of information."

"So, that's true?" Jonah thought for a second. This woman, who worked at the highest levels in the US government, was telling him that the earth was a fraction as old as he thought it was.

And he believed her.

"Ok. Let's say, yes, I believe that."

"Do you think that women have as high a sex drive as men?"

Jonah looked up. "Traditionally, people say that men have much higher sex drives than women do. I mean, traditionally."

"How about with you and Eve?"

"Well, we seemed, always, pretty evenly matched. Lately, she is a little wilder."

"What would women's sex drive be like if they were always safe?"

"Safe." Jonah thought. "Safe like in what way?"

Grey took a beat. "Ok. step back by that wall."

Jonah took a step back.

Grey lifted her right hand out of the water and slapped him across the face. Jonah looked stunned. He hadn't expected that. She pulled her hand back again and let go.

This one was even harder. She put her left hand forward and grabbed his nipple, twisting it hard. He grimaced and shut his eyes. He put his hands on the wall behind him.

"Open your eyes. Stay here."

She pulled her hand back and hit him again and again and again. Jonah's face burned red hot as he counted. 25 slaps.

She stopped, holding her hand. She placed it under the water and looked into Jonah's face.

He was crying. Tears filled both sides of his face as the one side turned red. Grey held his head while he sobbed, smoothing down his hair.

"Are you ok?"

"Yes sir,"

"Safe. No matter what I do to you, you'll never once try to hurt me. You won't ever say no to me. You'll do what I say, no matter how much it hurts you. You'll never raise your voice to me or put me down. You'll never pretend to be better than me or deny me anything. You'll never stop me from doing what I want or prevent me from taking from you."

"Yes, Sir."

"You'll never push me or try to get something from me. You'll care for me, you'll protect me. You'll never lose your temper or be seen disagreeing with me."

"Yes, Sir."

She whispered to him. "I'm safe."

She continued, "And I'm incredibly turned on. I feel smart. I feel powerful. I feel unstoppable. That's me feeling safe."

Jonah lifted her right hand from the water. It was red and raw but beautiful. He kissed it.

"You willingly kissed the hand that beat you."

Jonah nodded.

"Do you see what that kind of safety does to us?" She kissed him. Deeply and with a wide open mouth. She explored his mouth with her tongue.

There was love in it.

"Come here." She lifted him up until he was sitting on the edge of the pool. She spread his legs and licked the tip of his dick. She took her time, feeling how it felt on her tongue before opening her mouth and letting it inside. She sucked, marinating his cock in her mouth, knowing it would stay soft. There was no pressure, no time, no urgency.

Jonah felt the strangeness of it. Her mouth was amazing, warm, soft. And it felt so good. But there was a disconnect, somehow. No matter how good it felt, he knew he would not get hard.

He couldn't cum.

She played with him with her hands and mouth, stuffing his flaccid prick and balls into her mouth the whole way. For a moment, he was embarrassed by the slight size of his manhood, soft, unerect. No one had ever given his soft prick so much attention, seen it and played with it so small.

He closed his eyes. No matter how hard he tried, he couldn't thicken, harden. A part of his mind panicked and he reminded himself over and over that the medication was temporary.

Her mouth was wet and sloppy on him and her saliva dripped down between the crack of his ass and down his thighs. She rolled him over and licked his ass, fucking it with her tongue. It felt incredibly dominant from her, strangely. He tried to relax, letting his ass open as she pumped her tongue into him. It felt open and sloppy and he knew that he had more than one load of cum in there over the last few days.

He thought of his ass, just then, as a primary sex organ, equal to his cock, for giving pleasure.

She pulled him back down. Eve had slid into the pool while he was turned away. She was sucking on a server who was sitting on the edge of the pool. As Jonah turned around she dove toward him, kissing him, her mouth filled with cum. Jonah was happy to see her again, more than he even thought she would be. This was all still so strange to him.

Grey waved away the server. He shot up and rushed away as Grey slid into their embrace. She whispered to Jonah. "Now I'm going to tell you something that very few men on earth know."

He pulled back, holding onto Eve's waist as she continued.

"This world has less than a year left."

Chapter 10

It was fairly late when they got back to the apartment. Jonah had drawn a bath for both of them to sit in, together. It was less cramped than he thought and he suddenly wondered why they'd never done it before. Eve ran her fingers over his face.

"Ouch. Your face is going to be black and blue tomorrow."

"You are not wrong." His face felt tight, like it might break if he smiled. "Let me ask you a question."

She made little finger guns and shot him. "Shoot."

"Are you turned on all the time because you feel safe?"

Without a second's hesitation, Eve responded, "Yes. Next question."

"I make you feel safe?"

"Yeah. Completely, Jo."

The way she said that made Jonah sad he still couldn't get an erection.

She continued, "You've never raised your voice around me."

He thought, "Have we never fought?"

"Well." she splashed him. "We've disagreed."

Jomah tried to remember one time. He could not.

"What happened then?"

Eve laughed."I wore smaller shorts."

A little voice in Jonah's head said, "yup." Out loud he said, "Is that true? I mean it feels true. Am I shallow?"

"No, you just like me more than you like being right." She put her hands underwater and played with his flaccid cock. "It's so weird playing with it like this. How does this feel?" She massaged it, wrapping her hands softly around the shaft and balls.

"I mean, it feels great. Just nothing happens." It would be hours before the medication wore off.

"But it feels good."

"Oh, yeah?"

"Ok, Ima keep doing it."

Jonah thought. "I dominate you sometimes."

"Yeah. When I want. When I beg you to. Would you ever think of it if I didn't ask you? Would you ever consider hurting me if I didn't beg you?"

"No. Not at all."

"It wouldn't be fun for you, would it?"

Jonah felt strange. Did Eve just know everything about him? "No. But it's always fun when you attack me."

"All the times when I'm an animal and I rip into you? Like when I scratched your face? When I made your ass bleed so much? When I crouch down and growl and drip all over the place? You never did anything but drop your hands and take it."

Jonah nodded.

"Why do you think so?"

He was having some trouble thinking while she played with him like that. Then it came to him, "Because being wanted by you is everything."

She nodded. "Bingo."

"So, you feel safe and I feel wanted."

"And that's why I'm wetter than this tub all the time."

Jonah sighed. If that didn't make him hard, nothing would.

"I went upstairs with that guy and we rolled around and sucked each other like three times. He shot in my mouth, then rode me and shot in my pussy and then climbed on me and ripped my ass open with his beautiful dick. I got every bit of cum out of that guy. Seriously, probably forever."

Jonah spread his legs a bit. "I'm glad you had fun."

"And still, the hottest part of all of it was telling you that now."

"Oh, yeah?"

Eve leaned in and kissed him. "It would be no fun being a whore if I couldn't show you or tell you."

"You know I've been pretty slutty, too lately?"

"I know." Eve kissed him.

"Not to brag, but I've actually had a lot of dick."

"I know I'm starting to get worried you're going to get knocked up." Eve Laughed.

"Oh, oh, did you know Marissa has a breeding fetish?"

"Did you put a baby in her tummy?"

"I tried." He felt so close to Eve. He felt lucky. "Do you want to do anything to me before we go to bed?"

"Will you sleep with your face in my pussy?"

He kissed her and padded into the kitchen, turning up the thermostat to 80. They hadn't done this in a while, but when they moved in together, they discovered it was fun to sometimes turn the heat up all the way and sleep above the covers, his face propped up by her open cunt. And if the temperature was warm enough, Eve would be sweaty and sopping by morning.

He tucked in next to her and slept

***

Marissa was mean and sarcastic the next day, barking at him, even ordering him around in his own office. But Jonah could see it in her eyes.

She was having fun.

There was a half smile on her face that even Keith recognized. She called him an idiot and stood there while he slapped her ass. Without moving, she lashed out.

"Pussy."

Until he did it harder. She almost fell over and then returned to her desk.

Keith looked up from his computer. "Ok, she's kind of a ball."

"Is it weird that I think it's fun when she yells at me now?"

"I got a little crush, not gonna lie." Keith hit send on his computer. "And, I'm done for the day, unless you want to play project manager and reclaim those hours I'm about to waste."

"For the love of god, man, waste them. I think they're government hours."

Keith fistbumped the air. "Sweet. So you going to that other club tonight?"

"Archon, yes."

"With the little girl who's mostly pussy?"

Jonah cocked his head. "That's a weird way to put it. I'm just fascinated that there is a full sized cunt on this tiny woman. Like where do things even go?"

"You think she's bigger on the inside?"

"I'm not comfortable with this conversation."

Marissa walked back in. "You really are a pussy, then."

"Look, it's just weird. The human body is amazing."

Marissa nodded, "Some of them are."

Jonah smiled. "You should admit that you like me."

She looked at Keith, "He thinks that because I was crying, spreading my little whore legs begging him to put a baby in me that I must like him."

Keith pursed his lips, "It IS a sign of that, yes."

"I didn't tell him that, by the way." Jonah pointed to Keith.

"Are you embarrassed, little pussy, that you owe me an assfuck?"

Keith perked up, "Wait, you owe this hottie an assfuck? Fork it over, pussy."

"Oh, my god, you're supposed to be MY friend."

Marissa stepped over to Keith, "If you want some of this ass, you should come to the party."

Jonah put his head in his hands. "Oh my god."

Keith shot up. "Ok, I'll go."

Marissa smiled sternly. "Good. Jonah, you still need to bring someone."

Jonah's mouth dropped open. "Wait, I was going to bring him."

"Nope. I encouraged him to go. You need to bring a person to serve."

"Jesus."

"If not, you get the Elyx."

Keith looked scared, "Shit. What is that?"

Jonah looked over to him, "It's an electrical rod they shove up your ass that makes you cum on command."

"You are all crazy people."

Marissa patted him on the arm, "It wouldn't work on you. You don't have a prostate."

"So, I'm off the hook?"

"No, we just have different ways to torture men like you." Marissa smiled at him, grabbing his face.

Keith glanced over at Jonah, "She's kind of hypnotically hot."

"Yes, she's super hot, but she's really mean."

Marissa pushed him playfully. "Shut the fuck up, Jonah."

"Yes, sir."

She leaned on Keith's arm and reached under her skirt, pulling her black panties off. She placed them on Jonah's desk and walked out.

Keith paused for a minute. "If you don't want those, can..."

Jonah shook his head. "Shhhhh."

He grabbed them.

***

"What do you want to do tonight?" Jonah drove the two of them in his car.

Eve was next to him in a yellow dress. "Ha. It's up to you."

He whispered. "Eve. I think you have an idea."

She laughed. "Ok. how about only you hit me. But whore me out to anyone you want?"

That sounded new to him. He liked the idea that only he would hit her. He wasn't sure about how things worked here "ok. I'll keep you in sight."

"I want to see you with her." Eve put her hand on his leg. It felt so innocent. Like they were a couple of swingers.

They pulled up to Giselle's place. She pushed him out and waited in the car as he let himself in with Giselle's key and went up to the second floor, walking into her apartment. She was naked, from the shower, putting makeup on. She jumped when she saw him. He was a little early and she jumped

"Oh. sir. You scared me."

Jonah grabbed her by the tits and pulled her over, kissing her. She dropped her arms and hugged his waist as he twisted her nipples

She closed her eyes. "Yeah. More. Harder."

She put her hands behind her head as he twisted them harder, her smaller breasts twirling into shapes that looked like dishrags being twisted. She breathed heavily and pushed her chest out.

"Fuck. Fuck."

Jonah spit in her face. She opened her mouth as he did it again, swallowing in eagerly.

He let go of her tits and she dropped to the floor, licking his shoes. She picked them up, trying to lick the bottom.

He saw her naked ass as she crawled on the floor. She was so pale, bright pink between the legs. He helped her up and kissed her.

She kissed him back enthusiastically and started pulling her out of her apartment. She didn't bother to ask for her clothes as he pulled her down the stairs to the street entrance. Nobody was on the street but there was the occasional car. He looked and saw Eve leaning against the car in her dress. Eve saw Giselle was nude and pulled her own dress off in one fluid movement, standing there naked. She opened the back door and tossed her dress in.

Jonah dragged Giselle across the street and threw her in the back seat. She slid in legs first. Eve climbed in, crawling over her, putting her ass in her face as she started eating the smaller girl's cunt. Jonah slid into his seat and drove while the two women sucked each other like animals in the back seat.

As he drove, for a moment Jonah panicked that passing cars could see them. It turned out that the cars tall enough to see in the back window seemed to have no problem with it. One woman even winked at him.

By the time he pulled up to Archon, the car smelled like cunt, which was all that Jonah needed to see that his erection response was back to normal.

The parking lot was empty, but it wouldn't have mattered. He pulled the women out and held their hands as he made his way to the entrance. Eve kissed him, biting his lip. Giselle lowered her eyes and pulled in close to him as they entered the outside foyer.

Jonah pulled out his key and opened the door. Gerald was there, smiling and ushering him in. He was wearing a bright blue suit today and he looked taller than he even did last time.

"Mr. Gilden. Jonah. It's good to have you back."

Eve whispered in his ear.

Jonah leaned in and asked, "Gerald, do you have a marker and some rope?"

He nodded, checking to see the women were naked. "Yes sir. Let me get those." He looked in a drawer behind him and pulled out two lengths of black rope and a thick red marker. "Does that work?"

Jonah nodded and shook his hand. Gerald reached for Eve, shoving his massive meaty hand into her pussy to lift her on the table. For a minute, she seemed surprised, but then she put her head down. He put his elbow on her back and pulled out the tattoo gun, placing a single diamond on her inner thigh. He took his time and then slapped her ass, pushing her off the table. Jonah grabbed her and held her up as he shoved his hand into Giselle's ass, doing the same to her. He shifted, trying to dig his whole flat hand in her anus. She seemed to push her ass in the air to facilitate it.

He lifted her off the table and nearly threw her when he was done. It seemed like a needlessly cruel motion that almost guaranteed she'd fall. Eve reached for her and held her up. The two of them kissed and walked into the main area.

They moved past the pool table. As they walked more deeply into the club the spaces seemed to get more and more brutal. They passed a room where women were strung up from the ceiling being whipped, each showing the thin raw red marks of the whip all over them. They passed a room where women were locked into urinals, their faces and pussies propped open to the streams of men from all over the club. The stench was overwhelming and Jonah felt Eve shudder involuntarily.

They turned around and backtracked. Jonah looked for a place to do what he wanted to do. He found a perfect space not far from the entrance. There were two seats arranged next to each other. One, where a woman could be bent over and fucked by everyone from behind. The other where she would face her user, watch as he violated her. He nodded at Eve. She leaned in to him. "I want to see."

Jonah retrieved the rope and used one line to tie Giselle's arm to his She looked grateful to him for that. Maybe even wanted. But Jonah liked the look in her eyes.

Giselle helped him use the other rope to tie Eve up in the chair.

It forced her legs up in the air in a slightly more than 90 degree angle, exposing both her pussy and asshole. Her arms were tied downward, down the column, useless. Giselle bent over and gave her pussy and ass little kisses as Eve laughed. Jonah pulled out the marker and wrote, "Fuck me nice" on her. With "Fuck" on her forehead and "Me" and "Nice" on her tits. He had to admit that he had rarely been harder looking at her. She was so fucking beautiful. Even just her lips were the best thing in the room.

He reached between Giselle's legs and grabbed her clit. He loved how big it was, twisting it in his hand. She leaned into him in tremendous pain. But the pain was causing her hole to drip all over his hand. He looked at her. "Do you like that?"

She nodded, breathing like an animal, "Yes, sir. I love it."

Jonah said, loudly, so Eve could hear, "I'm going to keep twisting your clit until the first guy comes to fuck her. I might twist it off." Giselle looked at Eve.

It was clear she was in pain. Eve panicked and yelled out. "Please. Someone use my pussy. Anyone. Please." She scanned the room. The men seemed to be all involved in some kind of play. She yelled out louder, "Please, please fuck my pussy or my asshole or something. Please. I'll take anyone."

A larger man, hairy all over, walked past with his partner, a smaller woman, in tow. Eve called out to him.

"You, sir, please. Can you fuck my pussy or ass or something. Please. Come here, please."

Giselle was crying, her head lowering as she struggled to keep her legs open. Her breathing included the occasional sob.

The man stepped over, dragging his partner "I'll fuck your ass."

"Please, now, please, do it. Shove it in my ass."

He stepped up to her and droped his pants, massaging his cock.

He was nearly hard. Eve begged him, "please fuck me. My ass wants it so bad."

Jonah could see that her pussy was literally pouring out all over her ass. It would take very little to shove anything in that ass right now. Her hole seemed to be opening and closing, begging for it.

Giselle kissed Jonah's chest and he could feel her tears through his shirt. She started moaning loudly in one long sound. He held her up by her ass as she started sinking.

The hairy man finally got completely hard and pushed his prick into Eve's ass. She called out, gratefully as Jonah let go of Giselle's clit. "Thank you. Oh, god, thank you. Use that ass. That's right. Fuck it, please. Dump your fucking cum in it."

Jonah kissed Giselle, lifting her onto the table. She climbed up and leaned over to the seat where Eve was being fucked, grabbing her and kissing. Jonah could see that they were crying together. Giselle was kissing her while Eve was licking the tears off the smaller girl's face. They stayed connected at the lips as Eve moved back and forth with the force of the fuck.

The hairy man finished and two more men fucked Eve when Jonah finally tried to separate them. He pulled Giselle over and told her what he wanted to do.

"Ok, I'm going to take some time to screw you and then I'm going to take some of the items here hanging up and stretch out that crazy pussy of yours. What do you think?"

She nodded, excitedly and kissed him. "Thank you, sir. I can take a lot."

Jonah continued "I really want to see how stretched out we can get it, ok?"

She nodded, happily.

So sometimes I'm going to reach into your ass and measure or just feel how far they go into your tiny stomach. And make marks on you. OK?"

She nodded enthusiastically.

"Do you want to hold onto Eve while she's being used?"

She looked like she wanted to cry. "Can I? Please? I'll be good."

Jonah nodded. "Let me know if anyone hurts her, ok?"

Giselle wrapped her arms back around Eve and held her. "I promise. I will."

The two of them seemed inseparable. Giselle held on tightly as Jonah pulled a baseball bat off the wall and slapped her ass. Slowly he inserted it into her open cunt, large side first. It slid in easily.

She slobbered all over Eve as he felt it through her belly, pushing it as far as it would go. He drew a line where it ended, under her ribs. It was unbelievable. Jonah tried to remember what he knew of anatomy. Giselle was a miracle. He slipped his hand into her cunt and then dipped it into her ass. He pushed deeper, trying to feel the bat as it disappeared inside her. She squirmed, spreading her legs, pawing at Eve while a tall blonde man took turns fucking her cunt and ass. He could feel the bat so far up. Her ass and pussy were so open.

By the time they got home, there was cum pouring out of every one of Eve's holes and red marker lines up and down Giselle's belly. Even back in Eve and Jonah's bed, Jonah found he couldn't get the two women to separate. He fucked eash slowly as they hugged and kissed each other. Both of their cunts felt open and alive and sloppy wet.

At some point they all fell asleep.

Chapter 11

A story from the House of Love

En-Saddiqa and Apollyon

Millions of years ago, when the planet was young and green and people were unashamed of who they were, they worshiped the goddess of fertility and lust, Alitha.

Alitha was a kind goddess, aware of what excesses her people's hot blood drove them to every day, the passions, the power of skin on skin contact, the sheer enormity of physical love. She was committed to fertility, but realized that the hurricane squall that made up sexual attraction was a force that powered all human interactions. She was the inclusive goddess for every touch, every errant glance in the bathhouse, every impassioned breath where a name was said, or two, or three. And when people closed their eyes to touch themselves at night, minds full of chaotic sexual thought, she was there, each time, collecting their joy, their passions, their strength, and building on it.

Because of that, Alitha had other gods in her retinue. Some who followed her around, available at a moment's notice. Some who saw her only rarely, engaged as they were with the diversity of the sexual experiences of the people who worshipped them. And, as the world wore on, she birthed ever new gods, whose novelty drove those experiences powerfully.

And one day, Alitha caught the eye of Solara, who was also called Auroketh, the sun goddess. She reveled in her dynamic presence and enjoyed the feel of her eyes on her bare skin as she went about her day. They flirted more and more openly. Until one day, Alitha went down to the earthen beach and removed all her clothing, Alitha placed her clothes on the ground and bent down, showing the sun the curve of her back and the raw pink of her asshole between her spread open cheeks.

She rolled on the ground in supplication, laughing and worshiping the errant light rays that spread all over her. She flirted with an intensity and passion that left her dripping wet on the ground. Then, She placed her fingers in her cunt and opened it like a flower for the beams of Solara to enter. And, excited and empowered, he did, again and again, spilling vibrant golden sunshine inside her where she kept it, happily, for 9 months, until giving birth.

The child who was born to them, En-Saddiqa, was beautiful and gifted and, even as a young child, could speak in such a way that people of all kinds listened and were often entranced by. It soon became clear that the child would grow up to be special, unique even among the gods, with the ability to create safety in her words, to make liberty out of compliance to her desires. She would one day become one of the major gods in Alitha's retinue - the god of Dominance.

When people wished to experience the nurturing flame that enveloped them, physically, to be adored and directed, to be tied down and made pretty by the eyes of their own goddess, they prayed to En-Saddiqa, who, if enamored of their prayer, would fill them with the true spirit of servility and send to them an owner, a master, someone who could make their flesh burn but heal it at the same time. Someone who could see how they most wanted to be used by the world and present to them the satisfaction of that use.

For centuries, Alitha relied on her child, En-Saddiqa to help inflame the passions of her followers, to hold down willing paramours in beds of simple grass, hands around their necks, as they accepted the fluids of their lovers. People prayed to En-Saddiqa often and vigorously.

And when those prayers were met, they gave gracious thanks as they played in the vast playground spaces of the beautiful women, their men, non binary ones, and those who contained multitudes, directing them to pleasure.

but she soon saw that she was sad. As much as she loved what he did, she was without a precious flower of her own to worship and bless with her imperious nature. En-Saddiqa would often visit the people and give them what they desired, playing off their most servile and giving nature. But he knew that each was a tiny flickering flame, beautiful, but prone to grow old before his eyes, frail, and soon gone.

Alitha gathered the other gods and told them what she saw. She brought together every deity in her retinue to help solve this problem. And asked them all to bring something.

Nadira, the goddess of intimate pain, brought a rose bush, whose thorns and nettles had scraped the skin of a thousand thousand of her followers as they made love in beautiful pain. She placed it on the ground in front of Alitha.

Baraketh, the hermaphrodite god(ess) of elegant androgyny brought a knife whose blade would never hurt but would cut and reshape pieces of lovers' flash to mold them into anything they wanted to be, any golem of pure beauty they saw in their mind. They placed it on the ground

Mikada, the god of the pleasures of the mouth, brought a special mint, an intoxicating mixture that made the skin tingle and obsess for the feel of a tongue. She laid that at their feet.

And Tandemuth, the Goddess of wanting, brought, with her, a cream made from the pussies of a thousand beautiful women, each more desirable than the last, each cunt feeling like home, looking, for all intents and purposes, like the most desirable of all places to warm yourself at night, each smelling like the very wind of a night filled with promise.

And the other goddesses brought, each, one thing that would be used in Alitha's machinations. Alight looked at the score of goddesses standing before her and was pleased. She called En-Saddiqa to her side.

Using all the tools before her except one, she shaped a beautiful mold- a person - whose eyes were alive and bright, whose lips were full and smooth, and whose appearance would inflame anyone's passion. She turned to En-Saddiqa and told her.

"This is Appolydon, your slave now and forever. They will endure pain endlessly, as can be seen in this rose bush. They will never fail to beg to have you in their mouths, as attested to by this gift of Mikada. And they will beg for the release of your touch, always."

En-Saddiqa was pleased and asked Alitha which of the gifts she still held in her hand. She showed her the blade of Baraketh and gave her the last of the true gifts.

"With this blade, you can determine always how Appolydon will best serve you."

En-Saddiqa reached out to Appolydon, whose manhood lay between their legs. With her blade, she removed it, placing it in her pocket. Appolydon stared into his eyes with approval and delight, spreading their legs wide. Appolydon's hands slid behind their back to better serve and open up to their beloved owner.

En-Saddiqa dug in his blade and made a beautiful opening between Appolydon's legs, just large enough to accept anything she wanted. And then En-Saddiqa laid them down as the assembled gods all wrapped themselves around this new slave and each entered them, bestowing the best of all their aspects- using them without respite.

From then on, En-Saddiqa shaped her most adored one as she most wanted that day. Some days, she returned to the beloved god his manhood and placed it in such sublime pain that Appolydon cried into the softness of their owner's neck. Some days, he cut deeper, opening up Appolydon's servile cunt to the pleasure of his friends and even, sometimes, the people who worshipped him.

Some days Appolydon spent not knowing how they were to serve that day, while some days the depth of that service was visible at first light.

And when En-Saddiqa hurt them deep into the night, with love and the intensity of true adoration, Appolydon's godly aspect would find them fully healed in the morning, begging their owner to try, once again, to make them whole through their passion, to take any part of them needed that day through Baraketh's blade, and to create, for them, the kind of pain that would never leave them wanting, for the next thousand years.

***

"That was amazing." Giselle sat on the couch, eating an egg sandwich Jonah had made. They were all nude. The difference was Eve and Jonah had clothes. Earlier, she had asked if she should put a towel down if she sat on the couch. Eve laughed and Jonah loved that. They weren't that kind of household.

"We were clean, but horny," Jonah thought.

Jonah sat on the floor, listening to Eve. "It really is. How have I never read this?"

Eve lowered the book. "It's not really ready."

Giselle grabbed for it, "But it's a book. It's beautiful. It's like a kind of foreign mythology. I want to read it."

Jonah agreed. "Yeah me, too."

Eve smiled, "Will you guys give me some time?"

Jonah crawled over and put his head near her lap. "Yes, sweetheart."

Giselle leaned over and kissed her. "Well, I think it's as beautiful as you are. I'll wait. And then you have to take my money." She dug her face into Eve's neck and she giggled.

"Look, no one's working today. You want to see how long we can go before we go near an article of clothing?" Eve laughed.

"Ooh, I do. You have the best boobs, though. I'm like flat next to you." Giselle covered and uncovered her breasts. They were small but lovely, Jonah thought.

"Did you have fun last night?" Eve asked her.

"I did." She smiled.

Jonah asked. "What did you like, what didn't you like?"

"Um. Well. There was nothing I didn't like, really. I thought I'd have a heart attack when you just let yourself in. But after a second, it was so hot."

Eve asked, "You liked being broken in on?"

"A lot. Would you use the key, too? Like in the middle of the night sometime?"

Eve laughed, "Do you want me to?"

"Fuck yeah. I want both of you to." Giselle leaned back and spread her legs. Jonah loved how comfortable she seemed.

"When he was twisting your clit and you were in pain, I was so desperate to stop it I just begged any loser to come fuck me. It was crazy. I panicked. I needed to save you. It was such a crazy feeling." Eve seemed to be getting turned on just talking about it.

Giselle breathed out heavily, "I know. It hurt so bad. And it made me love you so much that you did that. Like you were sacrificing yourself for me. It was amazing. And when he stopped, I fell in love with him." She pointed to Jonah.

Jonah smiled mischievously, "So, do you still really like her?"

Giselle rocked back and forth. "Oh my god. When I look at you, that's all I can think. You saved me." She leaned in and kissed Eve with her mouth wide open.

Jonah reached over and caressed her inner thigh. "So these are all from Archon?"

She fingered them, spreading her legs wider. "Yep. I'm almost at ten. My ex boyfriend, Paul, said that at ten he would tell me some big secret. Then he went away."

Jonah kissed them. "Do you know where he went?"

She looked at him and bunched up her face. "No. I don't. He didn't call, didn't anything. He had a key, too. He knew where to find me."

Eve pulled her over under her arm, "I'm sorry, sweety." She kissed the top of her head. "Do you like it there?"

Giselle thought. "At Archon? I like what happens there. I like being used. I love being wanted. I think last night might have been my favorite time there."

Jonah smiled. "That makes me happy." He pulled her over and kissed her belly.

She giggled. "That makes me have to pee. " She started to get up.

Eve held onto her. "Why don't you pee here?" She looked at Jonah. He nodded.

"What do you mean?"

"Have you ever peed in someone's mouth?" Eve kissed her.

"I've had men piss on me. I like it. I've never done it the other way."

Eve licked her ear, "Do you want to do it with Jonah?"

Giselle was squirming again, crouching down on the couch with her legs spread. She moaned and leaned into Eve's tongue. "Does he want to?"

"He wants your piss so bad. Jonah loves women, right, sweetheart."

Jonah kissed Giselle's belly. "I do. So much."

"I've never been a top like that."

Eve pulled her legs apart further while Jonah turned around and leaned his head back under her.

"Now lean forward and put your hands on his chest. Can you do that?"

Giselle closed her eyes, feeling Eve's lips on her neck and ears while Jonah placed his tongue at the opening of her urethra. "I can. Like this?"

"Perfect." Eve kept kissing her, putting one hand on her belly. "Do you feel his tongue licking your little pee hole?"

"I do. It's really good. Are you sure this is ok?" Giselle seemed hypnotized by Eve's voice and tongue on her. "Oh, it's really good."

Eve rubbed her belly. "Can you tell how much he wants it?"

"I can feel it." She ran her hands over his chest. "His tongue is so nice."

"Are you almost ready to pee?" Eve whispered, her tongue in Giselle's ear.

The smaller woman moaned, "I am. I have to. It's too much."

Eve bit her ear. "It's ok. He can take it."

"Oh, my god I'm ready. It's so much."

Eve moaned back at her. "Ok, when i kiss you on the lips, so soft, I'm going to press on your belly. And you will start to pee in my boyfriend's mouth ok, baby?"

"Oh. my god. I'm so in love with you."

Eve kissed her cheek, on the way to her lips. She pressed down on her belly as she took Giselle's lips in her and let her tongue flit inside, exploring her mouth."

At that moment, a stream of piss flowed out of her into Jonah's open mouth. He clamped onto her vulva as she clamped her mouth onto Eve's. She pawed at her and shivered as she let loose. Jonah swallowed over and over, quickly. He had learned, when doing this with Eve, that he needed to swallow while his mouth was filling up, rhythmically.

It was definitely a skill, especially if you didn't want to leave a huge mess.

When she finished, Jonah cleaned her up, licking all over her vulva. She settled back and kissed Eve deeply. He dug his nose between her labia and licked at her clit. He really liked how large her clit was. He could feel it easily with his tongue. He could suck on it like a litte dick and he could work it in his mouth.

She rubbed her asshole on him and moaned as he sucked on her clit. She was still squatting down when he heard her moans become more bassy, deeper, and felt the light release of her cum, flowing from her cunt, covering his face. She yelled out and Eve laughed.

"Oh, fuck, fuck. I just came so hard." Jonah heard her as he relaxed, letting her rest on his face.

Evie laughed and asked her, "Was that fun?"

"You guys are so great. That was wonderful. I can't believe I pissed in someone's mouth. She slid off Jonah's face and started kissing him. "Are you ok?"

Jonah laughed, "Yes, sweety, I'm fine. I abused you pretty badly last night, are you ok?"

Giselle giggled, licking the piss off of him. "Yes, I wanted it really bad. I love being hurt by you."

Eve slid onto the floor to join them. "What do you do for a living?"

Jonah laughed. "I think she's a doctor."

Giselle looked shocked. "Oh my god. How did you know that?" She turned to Eve. "I'm an ER doctor."

Eve looked at Jonah impressed.

He shrugged, "I have like 20 pictures of her in a doctor's lounge, stripping off scrubs and showing off her pussy and ass."

"I have not seen all of these pictures." Eve laughed.

Giselle leaned over and peppered Eve's belly with tiny kisses. "I have more for you."

"Can I ask you a question?" Eve whispered.

Giselle nodded.

"If the whole world were like Archon, where men could do whatever they wanted to you, would you like that?"

Giselle breathed out, letting her lips flap like a horse, "If all the guys were like him, yes, definitely, 100%. Otherwise, I don't know. A part of me says yes. Like I want to, I want to submit and be objectified and used. I like being furniture, I like being a fuckdoll. I like being used and then going back to work. But I've met some horrible people there. So. I don't know."

Jonah thought about when she had asked her that. He realized that it depended on the people, too.

It depended on Eve.

"Did you like dominating Jonah like that?" Eve asked.

"Well. It felt amazing. It felt freeing. It was hot. But I didn't feel like I was dominating him. When he pissed on me, at Archon, I totally felt that he was dominant. But..."

Eve glanced over at Jonah. "Are you okay with this conversation?"

Jonah felt confused. Why wouldn't he be? "I'm fine."

"I know that Giselle has been kind of your plaything and all, is it ok if I mentor her?"

Jonah laughed, "Of course."

Eve kissed Giselle's hand, "Do you think we could date her together?"

Giselle looked so happy. It was strange that she had asked Jonah. He thought back to something that Marissa had said, just yesterday.

"Eve, do you own me?" Jonah took her hand.

Eve looked torn for a second. She looked into his eyes, trying to figure out if this was the time. Jonah saw her breasts rise and fall as her breathing got heavier.

She liked the question.

Jonah felt more naked than he ever had. He looked at her eyes, fiery, alive.

"I want you to own me."

She put her hand on his head, smoothing down his hair. He dropped his eyes and saw the glistening wetness of her perfect cunt.

"Then I do."

Chapter 12

It was called Usagi, or "Rabbit" in Japanese. Mostly because it was first discovered at the Japanese Misagu Observatory in Tokyo and it looked a little like a rabbit hunched over. It was .27 km long and made of rare metals, some found on earth and would touch down in 10 months in the Pacific Ocean, far from any significant land mass

If you believed the news, the government was 100% sure that the impact would not be sufficient to cause much damage, even to Pacific Islands like Fiji, Japan, and Hawaii. They had begun to set up cameras to record the tsunami height waves, most of which would dissipate completely by the time they hit the mainland.

The waves would lift the water levels worldwide for weeks, all across the globe, but, again, not enough to really cause any problems for anyone. And the turbulence in the oceans would cause winds that would lower temperatures in various waterfront areas for the same amount of time.

Probably a couple of weeks.

Essentially, it would be a great surfing season, but not much more.

Giselle waved her glass around. They had been in the house, naked, for two days and while she wasn't drunk, she was definitely feeling the wine. "So, it's like a nothing burger, right? Nothing is going to happen? The news used to be special."

Eve shook her head and turned off the TV, where the young female reporter was detailing the specifics of the asteroid.

She ran her hands through her hair and picked up her glass. "To the big fucking weird rock?"

Jonah toasted the big fucking weird rock as well. Then he poured a little wine into Eve's belly button as she sat relaxed on the couch and began licking it out. Eve and Giselle laughed. Everything tasted better off of Eve.

Everything.

Giselle was leaning back on the other side of the couch. She had propped her legs up on Eve's shoulder and from his position, Jonah could see her pussy between her crossed legs. She lifted her glass, "To being paid for doing nothing." She looked around. "I'm actually on call right now in the ED. This city's been so dead recently, though. It's like everyone wised up and stopped stabbing themselves with wine openers and shoving shampoo bottles up their asses."

Eve petted Jonah's hair. "To Wisdom." They all took a drink. Eve scanned the room. "Guys, if this asteroid were the big one - if it destroyed the world, what would you want to do? With your last days?"

Jonah looked up, "You're right. Because that's how we should be living, right? Like everything could be over tomorrow."

The smaller woman raised her glass. "That's easy. I'd spend it with you guys. Every day. Is that weird?"

Eve laughed. "Then move in. I'm starting a harem."

Jonah smiled at her. "You are? This is the first I've heard of it."

"Do you want her here?"

"Well. Yes."

"I think this is fun. We have a big bed. We can tie you up in it at night."

"Are you serious? Because I would love that."

"ARE you serious?" Jonah hadn't expected that.

"Sure. She's demonstrated she's potty trained."

"I really am." Giselle took a drink. The idea of being tied up every night was clearly intoxicating to her.

Eve turned to Jonah. "Ok. World is ending. What do you want to do?"

"Well. not be a project manager. Not work"

She nodded. "Ok."

"I would be with you. Maybe write a little. I don't know. I'd have fun. Is that stupid?"

Giselle shook her head. "Not at all."

Eve pulled him closer with her legs. The leggings she wore as her only clothes were soft and fuzzy. Jonah realized, suddenly, that he sat on the floor so often when she was on the couch so her cunt would be at eye level. Just as Giselle's was. This was the spot, apparently. He leaned in and kissed Eve's pussy and felt her wetness on his nose.

"Would you be fulfilled not working?"

"Ha. You're a writer. She's a fucking doctor. I'm a project manager. This is as close as you can get to babysitter. So…"

"That's good to know. Why don't you quit?" Eve winked. She played with his hair and spread her legs a little more for him and he inhaled her scent.

"Fuck, I wish I could. I need to pay my way. I have a hot girlfriend. And it looks like SHE has a hot girlfriend."

"Who can both pay their own way. Don't use me as an excuse to not quit. I say quit your job." Eve pushed him, challenging him.

"Ok, Miss speedy decisions. What would you do? Last day on earth?"

She pulled him over. "Do you really want to know?"

Jonah laughed. "I think I do, especially now."

Eve slid off the couch and crawled, forcing him backward. "I would hunt you. I would lock all the doors so you couldn't escape and I would hunt you and take you." She was breathing harder. There was pure desire in her eyes and it drove Jonah crazy. She grabbed his head roughly and pulled it down on the ground, straddling his face. "Look at this perfect pussy and ass. You let 13 losers fuck these holes, do you know that. They slobbered all over me and forced their pathetic meat in me. In my perfect holes."

Jonah started to breathe harder. "I'm sorry, goddess."

"That's right. I'm a goddess. And you let those pigs in me. You let them pump their useless cum in me like they deserved it. They slobbered all over me, kissed me, fucked me."

Giselle cut in, "Hottest girl they ever fucked."

Jonah chuckled a little, "No matter what, anyone who fucks you it's gonna be the hottest girl…"

"Shut the fuck up, Jonah."

For a second, Jonah was afraid she might actually be angry. But he recognized the movement of her hips while she dragged her wet cunt over his face. He wanted to let go, but she was fascinating. He was watching Eve literally turn into an animal.

"What do you want me to do?" He let his nose slide into her open hole, feeling her drip onto his face.

"Put your arms and legs out, spread 'em out." She barked at him.

Could Eve have been really upset? Jonah wished for a moment he could just talk to her. But she seemed to have become a different person. He realized she loved to have her power in public.

And Giselle was watching.

"Yes, Goddess." He spread out his arms and legs.

"Kitten, come here. Force your ass in his mouth, make him eat you."

Giselle jumped up and slid over, pushing her asshole onto his face. He started digging his tongue into it, licking it. He felt himself becoming an animal, too. Giselle put one knee up, spreading her asshole even wider. Her bottom was thin and without much padding, but it was a beautiful ass. He devoured her, letting himself go.

"C'mon. Eat that. Suck my little ass, Jo. It feels so good. Eat my fucking hole." She was quiet, timid. For Jonah, somehow it made it hotter. She was putting on a show for Eve.

Suddenly he felt a hand between his legs. It was rude, rough. It pulled up his dick and he felt a shot. It felt like the shot he had gotten at Sylo.

But something was different.

A red hot warmth poured through him. Giselle slid off him and he saw Eve kneeling over him with a hypodermic.

"Can you feel that?"

His cock grew hard. It was harder than he'd ever felt it. It felt thick and exposed. It was heavy, pointing upward, like a muscle between his legs. His balls were warm and tight.

"What did you do?"

Eve pushed his head down. "So, here's the deal. You know what this is. But you don't have an Elyx to push a button. So you need to fuck to cum."

His hand went down to his dick. He started stroking it. It felt impossibly good. But there was an urgency.

He needed to get off.

Eve choked him. "I'm going to hunt you. She's going to help me. You can try and jack off but if I catch you, I'm going to tease you until it hurts. You can't hit us, push us, hurt us in any way. Do you understand?

"Yes."

She slapped him three times hard. "Do you understand?"

"Yes, sir. Sir. Goddess." Jonah kept pumping his cock as Giselle grabbed his arms and held them above his head. She sat on them, shoving them between her legs.

"Fuck." Jonah rocked his hips. It felt like his balls were filling up. He remembered them saying how this increased production of cum. He felt like he would explode.

He tried to pull away.

"Do not hurt her." Eve chided him. She felt his balls. They felt huge and heavy.

He started panting."Please. Please." He tried to roll. He wanted to rub his prick on the floor. Anything."

Eve grabbed his dick. He almost came the second she touched him. His eyes pleaded with her.

Eve looked at Giselle. "You can let him go, Kitty."

She let go and Jonah shot up. He jumped over the couch and started pumping his dick. Eve grabbed his neck and pulled him down, crouching over him like a tiger. She choked him, her cunt dripping onto his chest.

She was breathing hard. "Stop it, now. Stop it…"

He stopped jacking his dick and moaned. He closed his eyes as his throat closed shut. He let his arms fall to the side.

Through it all, he could feel his prick, thick and swollen. His testicles felt like they were about to explode. He tried to slow his breathing and submit to her.

She was so beautiful.

"Kitty, take care of it."

Giselle slid her fat cunt over his dick, straddling him and holding onto Eve. He started pumping himself into her in desperation.

Eve slapped his face, still choking him. "Do. not. move. Let her fuck you or you don't get it."

"Yes sir." he tried to spit out. She had never choked him this hard. He moaned. "Please."

Giselle slowly started rocking on his dick, sliding up and down. Her cunt felt like the most amazing thing Jonah had ever felt. He closed his eyes and let the feeling wash over him. He wanted her faster. He tried so hard not to move.

"Do. Not. Move. Bitch." Eve slapped him again, with every word. He was moaning each time he breathed out. His face was raw and all he wanted to do was cum.

But he wanted to kiss that hand. Her beautiful hand beating him.

"How's it going, kitty?"

"It's so good, Eve. He feels like he's going to pop. Do you want him to do it in my pussy?"

"Yes, my kitty. Why don't you let him cum."

She started riding him in earnest. She laughed.

Jonah screamed out, " Yes. yes, yes. Thank you. Thank you." He started pouring cum into the smaller woman. Eve watched him lose control completely.

Giselle yelled out. "It's so much…"

Jonah was breathing hard. Eve let go of him and stood up. She looked impossibly tall. Her cunt was dark, nearly purple, wet, waiting for him.

All he wanted to do was climb inside her.

All she wanted to do was to hunt him.

She kneeled down over him and kissed him. "Run."

He rolled off the couch and bolted for the bedroom, pulling the door behind him and locking it. He could already feel his balls filling up. If he could just relax for a second and jerk off he could maybe stop this feeling from being so intense.

He started pulling on his dick. Eve and Giselle knocked at the door. He jerked harder. Just as he started cumming, Eve pushed the door open and slammed into him on the bed, pushing him up against the headboard. He was cumming all over himself as she buried her head in his neck, biting him. He let his arms fall to his sides and tried to weather it. He felt Giselle hold on to his cock and keep it away from Eve's pussy, hovering over it.

He moved his hips involuntarily. Even put her fingers on his nipples and twisted them, licking his face like a dog. Jonah closed his eyes, awash in the red hot pain.

Eve growled at him. "You made me break the fucking door. What do you say?"

"I'm sorry, I'm sorry, I'm sorry."

"What's my name?" She bit his neck hard again as he tried to pull back. She twisted harder. "Don't pull away from me.

"I'm sorry, goddess. I'm sorry, goddess."

She put her hand between her legs and lifted it to his mouth. It was wet and glistening, slick, covered in her. She put it in his mouth and he hungrily sucked on it.

"Do you like that, bitch?"

Jonah nodded. Over and over. His balls filled up to bursting in Giselle's hand.

She did it again and he eagerly sucked it.

"Put it in your asshole, kitty." Jonah felt Giselle's ass close up around his dick as he tried to stay still. He was breathing in short gasps now.

"Slowly."

"Yes, Miss Eve." Giselle slowly fucked his prick with her smaller hole. She faced him, squatting over him.

Jonah's arms were still there, motionless, at his sides.

Eve pushed her hand deeper into his mouth. He panicked but she pressed deeper. He tried to open his throat for her. He tried to welcome her hand.

He wanted to just love her hand.

His orgasm was incredibly intense. Giselle cried out as she felt his hot cum up her ass. She laid down on his chest, his cock still spurting inside her, kissing his nipples.

Jonah gagged and spit up. Giselle reached up casually and tried to help him open his mouth wider. He was whimpering as he gagged, saliva pouring from his mouth in waves, even as his orgasm hit him again, sending more cum up Giselle's pretty ass. She bounced up and down on his still hard member, forcing the tip of it deeper inside her than should have been possible.

If Jonah had been able to look down or open his eyes, he would have seen the red marker lines on her belly, showing the impossible progress of the massive objects he had fucked her with, half faded testimony to the incredible bigness inside of her, a magnitude that rendered everything else inconsequential.

***

Jonah woke up with Eve's face inches away from him. Her leg was thrown over him like it was nearly every night they slept together. Giselle was asleep, her face buried between his legs, her arms tied behind her. He put his hand on her head.

Eve's eyes opened. "Hey, baby."

He smiled and kissed her on the nose. "I'm not a raging hardon machine anymore."

She laughed and caressed his face. "I gave you another shot."

"Thank you."

"I fucked you up first."

"I know. I feel it all."

"Are you ok?"

"Do I have to fix the door?" Jonah kept staring into her eyes.

"We can do it together, Bob the builder. But, yes, the door is super fucked up."

"That was pretty hot."

She smiled at him. "What did you like? What didn't you like?"

"Well. It was terrifying. That probably goes in both categories. Mostly like. You're like some kind of animal."

"I am. You have that effect on me."

"You like having an audience, don't you?" Jonah let his lips fall open onto her wet mouth.

"Ohmigod, I really do. She's great. I think I can make a little dominatrix out of her."

"You could make anyone into anything. But, yeah. I liked it. I'm in a lot of pain."

"You and me both, buddy." She licked his tongue and pulled him in for a kiss.

"Tell me the truth."

"Ok."

"That was quick." he laughed. "But seriously. Are you upset that I tied you up to be used by all those guys?"

"No, baby, I was just inventing things to fight you over. I told you to whore me out. I don't care about that. I mean, those guys were losers and my cunt is a holy temple…"

"It is."

"But, no. I told you to do that. And I like that feeling when one guy gets off and the next guy climbs on. It's hot." She kissed him on the nose. "You're getting more comfortable with all of this?"

"I love exploring with you. It's been pretty great."

"It has been." Eve scooted closer to him and hugged him.

"It's getting easier."

"What part?" Eve smiled, wrapping her arms around him.

"This is going to sound like it makes no sense. I've been lying here thinking about it."

"Just say it."

Jonah took a breath. "I feel powerful when you abuse me. Like, I can take it. I feel like I'm skydiving without a chute."

"Dangerous?"

"But that's the thing. I don't need one. I trust you. But I'm starting to trust me, too. I feel strong when I don't fight back. I feel like it's proof I'm strong. I can prove I'm a survivor by just letting you hurt me. I don't have to fight back. I don't have to push or hit or lash out. I'm good the way I am. And the stronger you get, the more vicious, it just means I'm strong."

"So you feel all that?"

"Is that right, do you think? Is that what's supposed to happen?"

"Maybe?"

"I'm so powerful when I submit to you. You're the hurricane and I'm the thing that can stand up to the hurricane."

Eve held his arms. "I like that. I like being the hurricane. And you are the strongest thing I know."

"I love you."

"I love you, too." She pressed her lips down on his hard. "And, Jonah. You have a month."

"What do you mean?"

"To quit your job. Give them a month"

"What?"

"A month's notice. To quit your job. You're quitting your job."

She kissed him.

"Goodnight, sweety."

Chapter 13

One Year Ago

Grey Shirra-Austen was a beautiful woman. There was really no doubt about it. She was sometimes quiet, sometimes seductive. She was a good friend, too, thought Paul as he arranged the chopstick holders in a row in front of him.

He and Grey had met at least once a week at this Chinese place across from work for the last five years. The atmosphere was only so so. But the food was amazing.

"What are you reading?" She leaned over and grabbed the magazine from the larger man.

"Do you ever get sick of working totally in the shadows?" He reached over and replaced it with a menu.

Grey read the opening paragraph. "In 2036, a host of medications like Twillerex, sybo, and vivarex solved intimacy problems around the world with a one two three punch against STIs, Pregnancy, and sexual dysfunction." She tossed the magazine back at him. "You know there's no such thing as a one two three punch. It's just one. And then two."

"Do you want to break cover and write a letter to the editor?"

"Nope. How's that menu, guy who comes here every week?"

Paul usually needed the menu anyway. Although he'd sort of lost his appetite.

"You aren't hungry?"

He looked up. The truth is, he was starving. He loved this place. He was just somewhere else. That made him laugh a little.

She shook her head, "You are insane. Do you want to talk about the email?"

Paul took a deep breath. He was tall, well over 6 foot 4. He had short cropped black hair and a chiseled face. The chest that inflated when he breathed in was impressive. "I really don't, but I guess I have to."

Grey sipped her soup. "You can't leave her. I mean, you can leave me, but you can't leave her."

"I can't take her. She's not strong enough. I mean, you can survive anywhere."

Grey smiled and grabbed a shrimp roll from the center of the table. "True."

"Honesty, I don't even know how to ask YOU."

She looked up at him from across the table. "So, don't ask."

He shook his head. "Just like that?"

"Just like that. I can get pips, if that's your concern. There's a party coming up Saturday. It's pretty extreme. Where you go, I'll go"

"I don't want you to have to do that."

She closed the menu in front of him and pushed it away. "What if I just want to be with you?"

Paul's eyes welled up. The truth was he wanted to be with her, too. Badly. She got up and moved to the other side of the table, sitting on his lap. She kissed his eyes, feeling the wetness on her lips.

"I do."

He put his arm around her. "I'm not an asshole."

She laughed and shook his shoulders. "Yes, that's why I worry about you."

Paul kissed her on the lips. Their relationship had begun just weeks after they had started working together. But it had intensified once they got the news.

It changed everything.

He leaned into the crook of her neck. I wish I could..."

Grey patted his head and rocked. "I know. I know. It's not how you're built."

She lifted his head and looked into his eyes. "I'm ready."

He shook his head, "Who's going to take care of her?"

"I'll find someone."

He started crying for real. "Someone, some random person? Both of you? I love you both."

"So shut up and take me, then. Take us both." She tried again to kiss his tears away. She thought about Giselle. He wasn't wrong. She was slight, breakable. Grey loved her, too, but...

She couldn't do this, could she? Where Paul was going was harsh. Raw. At times horrible. But he had no choice.

Giselle did.

"I'm leaving tonight. I don't want to see her again. Will you tell her?"

Grey looked down. She felt the inside of her thigh where a tiny new tattoo sat, still raw and peeling.

It didn't mean anything.

"She's going to hate you."

Paul lifted his glass of water. "Well. to not being an asshole."

Grey returned to her seat and lifted hers. "You know it's bad luck to toast with water."

Paul laughed. And then a little more. Grey stared at him until he finished. He took a gulp of water.

"I don't think luck matters when the world's about to end.

***

Today

Jonah got to the office early, beating both Keith and Marissa. He stared into space. He was still staring off into the distance when Marissa arrived. She was wearing a small black skirt with a pretty red top. He smiled to himself.

"You look very superior today."

She flashed him one of her half smiles. "You are early."

"Yep. I think I'm quitting today. I've been told."

Marissa shook her head. "No, you are quitting, technically in one month. You're putting your notice in today. Here is a copy."

Jonah looked at the letter she had dropped on his desk. It sure sounded like him.

A lot like him, actually.

"Can I ask you a question, Sir?" Jonah leaned back in his chair.

She turned around and sat on the couch, crossing her legs. The skirt was short enough that it created the illusion you could see under it. On anyone else, that would have been the attention grabber in the room. But on Marissa, it was just a battle.

Her pretty face. Her nearly perfectly rounded natural hair do. The ring in her navel you could only see when she raised her arms. Those breasts.

All of it.

"How far ahead of me are all of you?"

"You mean, in chess moves?"

He smiled. "Yes, if this were a chess game, how far ahead of me would you be?"

She leaned forward. "Let me ask you this. Do you think that you are on a different color team than we are?"

"I'm not?"

Marissa shook her head. "What does the queen do, on the chessboard?"

Jonah sighed and stepped in front of his desk, leaning back. "You, Eve, Grey, You're all so far ahead of me, I can't even see the finish line."

"Can you let us worry about that?"

Jonah pulled his hand from his pocket. In it was a tiny piece of broken machinery, about the size of a quarter. As soon as Marissa saw it, her eyes shot up to the far corner of the room.

"That's right. That's where it was."

She stood up and moved to the desk, putting her hand over the broken camera and sliding it into her pocket.

"You feel behind."

"I AM behind. A couple of days ago, Grey kissed me and told me the world was going to end. Yesterday, I discovered a totally harmless asteroid is going to hit the earth. What am I going to discover tomorrow?"

"Hasn't it?"

Jonah cocked his head. "Hasn't it what?"

"Your world. Ended. Restarted. Changed?"

"If I asked you to keep a secret from Eve, would you?"

Marissa shook her head. "No. I'm sorry."

Jonah sighed. "I wanted to read her book. I woke up in the middle of the night. It was there. I figured it would be ok if I ONLY read the part she read to us. Like that wouldn't be breaking a rule, right? That's not a violation?"

Marissa shook her head. "Maybe."

The passage she read to us, "Solara, who was also called Auroketh?"

"Yes?"

"It really says "Solara, along with her sister Auroketh."

"Ok. "

"Why would there be two sun goddesses?"

"I think you're focusing on the wrong questions."

"I wish I knew the right ones."

Marissa pointed to the letter from his desk. "I'm going to bring this to HR. I want you to hand it to me and call me sir."

"Hand you the letter?"

"That's all you have to do."

"Can I see you in your office today?"

Marissa shook her head curtly. "No. I'll see you at my party tomorrow." She held her hand out.

He picked up the letter and handed it to her. "Here you are, sir. Thank you."

She took it and started to walk out. As she reached the door, she turned back.

"Remember the right question."

Jonah thought. And remembered the question. What's the Job of the queen?

Marissa walked out.

Jonah's phone notification went off. He looked down to see the pictures.

"Jesus."

***

A couple of hours ago

Giselle stepped out of the car into the parking lot. "Are you sure you want to go in?"

Eve walked to her side and dragged her by the arm. "What are you afraid of.?"

"I can't imagine you here." Giselle leaned her head against her.

Eve stood at the door and took a deep breath. "How do we know anything unless we explore." She shoved Giselle into the door.

On the other side, it was bright white. Unlike the other clubs, this one was cold, clinical, clean. They stepped up to the table on the right and removed their clothes, folding them neatly. The man behind the table looked at them, motioning for them to turn. They both did. He pointed to the rules next to him under a simple sign that said "Madara".

1. No speaking

2. No noises

3. You are food, you are things.

4. 3 hours maximum

Eve shook her head. This was very different from both Yleros and Archon. And the man staring at them seemed very different. His skin was bright white. His hair was short and blackish blue, eliminating the possibility he was an albino.

So what was he?

He grabbed Eve one hand between the legs and the other on her neck. She panicked for a minute and was then laid flat on the table on her back like a piece of meat. The man reached inside her, inspecting her. He shoved his thin hand deeply into her, causing her to gasp. He put his fingers in her mouth and explored in that, as well, moving quickly without excitement. He pulled out a hypodermic and injected her directly below her breasts roughly. By this time, Eve was calm. She tolerated it. He rolled her over and spread her ass, staring into it. He spread her cheeks apart and reached inside her, again, inspecting her. She tried to slow her breathing as he pulled out the tattoo gun and placed a star on her spine. He then took a stencil and painted a glyph on her back, under the tattoo. Eve couldn't see what it was. He slapped her hard on the ass and rolled her off the table.

He then did the same with Giselle, dragging her like a slab of beef onto the table on her back and exploring her pussy and mouth. He inspected her, injected her, flipped her over, tattooed her and painted the glyph on her back. It looked like a letter, but nothing Eve had ever seen.

Eve's breasts began to feel heavy- so much so they were painful. She took Giselle's hand and they stepped into the inner door.

The room was filled with men and women - all pale and completely white, each with dark blue black hair. The space, though, looked like it might have been a restaurant. And each chair?

A naked man.

A couple of white-skinned people stood at the door. Each lifted one of them and walked toward the back of the space. There they saw what looked like about 30 women, swinging, arms and legs tied and hanging down, with milk pumps on their breasts that led to giant clear milk tanks. And in front of the tanks, people with stark white skin cooking, using milk from the tanks.

Eve had an idea of what madara was like, from Giselle, but it was so much more inhuman than she had imagined. The man walked up a flight of metal stairs to install her at the top. She looked around, trying not to lose sight of Giselle. He found an empty station and placed her on a floating table, facing down with her arms and legs hanging. He quickly tied her arms and legs so that she looked ready to walk on her knees and elbows. He pulled a rod out and inserted it into her ass to stabilize her, attaching it up top, and two pumps, one for each breast. A press of a button and she was lifted another foot or so, putting her mouth and cunt at waist level.

She couldn't move.

The shot, however, must have stimulated lactation, because as soon as the pumps were turned on, they began to suck milk from her breasts, slinking through a transparent hose, leading directly to the tanks.

Eve was not, however, prepared for how it would feel.

As the milk left her breasts, she felt a powerful rush, much like an orgasm. She started undulating, arching her back. She scanned the area to see Giselle and saw her, just a few people away to her right. Giselle was connected, as well, her smaller breasts pouring milk into the tubes - tubes that filled the tanks the cooks were using to make meals.

Eve felt her pussy twitch as the milk poured from her nipples. She had never realized how good it would feel.

Suddenly she realized the reason for the 3 hour limit

She arched her back and rocked back and forth. Looking to her right she saw Giselle bucking and undulating, clearly enjoying the sensation as well. She watched as a pale skinned man stepped over and slipped his cock into her pussy from behind, swinging her forward and back. She moved like a belly dancer, slowly and with a seductive grace, while the man seemed to fuck her with abandon.

She reminded herself to set up days, maybe even weeks, when only Jonah's cock could be in her. She looked forward to controlling who Giselle fucked. It would be like having another pussy that she owned.

Giselle was being screwed like a cow now in some bizarre animal porn cartoon. The man seemed to have no interest in looking at her or talking, just using her hole to get off in. As she watched, she felt a cock slip in her as well. It triggered a shudder through her entire body. She didn't realize how close to coming she had been, just from the stimulation until her clit began to vibrate. She didn't have any leverage of her own and tried to push back, letting the white man invade her and love her. He pushed her forward and she swung back over and over, impaling herself over and over as she rocked forward and back.

Another man appeared next to her face. She couldn't see anything but him slowly pulling his very white prick over and over. The man behind her was still fucking her, assuming it was the same one. And the sensation in her nipples seemed to be growing in intensity, if anything. She was breathing heavily, trying to push back on the dick up her cunt and wondering what the man would taste like when he finally came. Just as her own orgasm rose up, washing over her, the man in front of her grunted and sprayed hot white cum in her face. She opened her mouth and he slid his member inside, covered in ejaculate, still twitching. She felt the waves of her orgasm as she tried to service the rod in front of her. She licked at his cum and cleaned it, swallowing the man's oddly tasteless load.

It looked like a different man was fucking Giselle now and the sight of her trembling, cumming, triggered another climax for Eve.

She realized how hot she found it when the smaller woman came and filed that away for later play.

Every once in a while, one of the diners would look up and catch her eye. One or two waved at her. Eve wondered what was happening until One diner, eating on his own, lifted his plate along with a flag attached to it showing an obscure glyph.

It occurred to her that this was HER glyph. This symbol must have been the one on her back. And he was eating something prepared from her breast milk.

He was trying to tell her he was eating of her. He was calling out that they had a closeness. She saw diners waving at Giselle, their glyph matching hers. She wished she could go down and sit with the diners that were eating from her and be their date. She tried to wave back once as she was being fucked from behind but had no functionality in her arms.

It seemed like she had unleashed an impossible surfeit of breast milk into the tanks and felt her mouth grow dry. She heard a bell and a man inserted a penis shaped hose into her mouth, pouring water down deep inside her. She drank as much as she could and licked at the tip of the rubber. The water filled her up and her body converted it to milk. The last man had poured his cum into her and she waited for the next one to approach.

The room was eerily quiet and she made a point to follow the rules and to keep silent, despite the crush of her orgasms, amplified by the feel of the pumps on her nipples. It must have been time. A man, covered in white skin again, injected her in the ass with a hypodermic. Her breasts slowly settled and stopped lactating. He slid the devices off and let them drop on the floor as he slowly untied her, easing her to the ground and lifting her toward the door. Right outside the door, there were a row of chairs, each with a metal rod in the center. The man carrying Eve lowered her, spreading her pussy open roughly and docking her on the rod in the center of the chair. Giselle was let down next to her. It became clear that because of the height of the rod and the fact that her feet didn't reach the ground, she couldn't get off the rod until her arms regained their strength.

She was trapped.

Soon, her arms became less like rubber bands and she was able to push down, freeing herself. She helped Giselle step away from the seat, too.

Up on the wall in front of them, was a board with pictures taken of each of the "donors." She pulled her phone out and shot the picture of herself and Giselle, texting them to Jonah.

And they slowly moved to the car.

Chapter 14

The Birth of the house of Love

Keliosis, the great empty, had no gender and no form. But in its quiet expanse, it had birthed unmoving giants and godlike star systems, plants, stars, suns and moons.

Al of these efforts seemed part of the urge, born within the empty itself, to not be alone, to connect with something outside itself. It was a powerful drive, one that the void could not ignore,

But even as the great empty created, like an artist, it felt the pain of the artist, the loss, the sense that nothing was good enough. And while the empty cherished the solid and static children it had brought into the world, it sometimes wished that the urge to create- to have something outside itself - could be gone.

So it reached inside itself and pulled at that urge in order to purge itself.

Finding a lump inside itself it pulled and felt the lump dislodge. The great empty placed the lump on the sand in front of it.

The lump soon grew to the size of a baby. A baby so beautiful that she was hard to look away from. Her aspect had a silvery, elegant sheen. She stood up and continued to grow and, within short decades, achieved her true final form, that of Alitha, the goddess of lust, wanting, fertility.

Alitha was glorious. She was happy. She filled all the space around her with the endless joy of creation and passion. And soon, as it experienced her, Keliosis felt still her presence in them.

Because lust and the joy of creation- connection- was so great that even pulling out part of it could never dim its brilliance. Because a percentage of lust is all of wanting.

But the great empty felt even more than that. As it stared into Alitha's eyes, it realized how much it loved all its children, everything it had created. At that moment, another lump came to the surface of the thin area between nothingness and reality that was its skin. It pulled free another baby, another girl even lovelier and more beautiful than the first. This baby grew even faster and her countenance was gold and gorgeous. She grew to become Myanho, the eternal goddess of love.

As Myano stepped toward her sister, it became clear to the void that there was even still, so much of her inside them, because love amplifies and builds with each use. they found that loving her made them love themself more, And the pain of creation began to soften and flow into one space inside them.

Keliosis knew what this pain was. It allowed itself to feel the space between themself and Alitha and Myanho. It let itself know that although they all lived in love that they would never again be the same entity, that this was as close as they could get. And that realization brought on a powerful feeling.

And the void pulled from itself the third and last lump and placed it on the sand. She was more beautiful than all, and her countenance was brilliant red, gold, intense, addictive to look at. The baby Mahatha grew to be the goddess of mania, the feeling of disconnection, of separation, the wild out-of-control madness.

But, as beautiful as she was, The great empty felt that feeling inside it lessen and become smaller. Because madness fades. For all its addiction and beauty and power, madness fades.

And it did.

The three sisters took each other's hands and together formed the first and brightest of all the houses, the house of love. And women everywhere would one day worship them and see them in their aspect.

Keliosis felt inside, still, that need to create, and that love for its creations, but the self hatred that made creation an act of pain faded more and more every day.

And when every bit of that hatred was gone, it began to create again in joy.

The mere presence of the house of love spurred the birth of all ephemerals. Ken sa Burra - The Goddess of Meaning, who was born from wonder at their very existence. Epiago - The Goddess of Knowledge and Truth, who found existence just through the verity of Love itself. Amana to Kina - the Goddess of Intuition and Beauty, whose form appeared in Love's ever moving shadow. And Horath Agada - the Goddess of Law and Death, who arose from nothing once the three sisters left the room.

And in their aspect, in the way they danced, in how they lived, they birthed the eternal twins, Cavi Curata - The Goddess of Beginnings and Cavi Ato - the winsome goddess of endings.

And that is how the house of Love built, at the foot of the great empty, the second and most wise House, the House of Ephemerals, to fill the imaginations of people forever and provide them with tools to speak, to learn, to grow.

**

Jonah read the pages again. This was part of the story from Eve's books, clearly. But why was THIS part in his desk drawer? He lifted Marissa's note. "That madness is a part of Love and Love comes before Law. See you soon."

When he had asked her to keep a secret from Eve yesterday, she had said she wouldn't. So that meant Eve wanted him to see this, too.

He glanced up in the corner. The camera was back, placed again.

But by whom?

The office was nearly empty today. Even Keith had taken a day. Jonah wondered if he would be at the party that night. He sat behind his computer, feeling lost.

A meeting request popped up on his screen. Two O'clock in Marissa's office.

He had asked to see her yesterday but she'd said no. Today she sent a meeting request. This was her asserting dominance.

He did some busy work in the meantime. He'd never given a month's notice for leaving a job before. He had wrapped up most of his work in a day or two. Now he was establishing best practices for his replacement.

If there was one.

Seemed a little intrusive, though, if he had to be honest. Was he a busy body? He had honestly never asked himself that question.

No one from HR had contacted him. He wondered if he would just stop getting money deposited in his account and that would be that. It seemed like an unsatisfying ending to a career. Maybe he had overplayed with Eve how badly he wanted to quit. He never thought he'd go out with such a whimper.

What would he do?

He pulled his phone out and texted Giselle.

Ass picture immediately.

The dots flashed on the screen and she sent a picture. It looked like her ass in a cafeteria.

Had she dropped her pants in the middle of lunch with coworkers to send him a picture?

That was amazing. Jonah thought she might be some kind of a superhero.

As it approached 2, he closed up and headed to Marissa's office. He hadn't seen her all day.

He thought about Giselle's obedience as he stood in front of Marissa's office. He sighed and removed his clothing, folding them all neatly in his hands. He looked over at the clock on the wall. At exactly 2pm, he knocked.

He heard her voice from inside. "Come."

Jonah took a deep breath and stepped into her office, closing the door behind him.

She was leaning against her desk in the middle of her office, looking down, writing on a clipboard. She had on a pair of boots and a black frilled shirt Jonah could see through.

Besides that, she wore nothing else. Her pubic hair looked soft and full and her hair was in an afro, a perfectly round shape. Her makeup was iconic. She looked up and saw Jonah, putting the clipboard down and motioning him over.

He dropped to his knees and began crawling to her. She crossed her arms underneath her breasts and crossed her legs at the ankle, waiting for him to approach. He crawled closer and saw her move the tips of her boots almost imperceptibly.

Jonah dropped his face and began licking her boots, making sure to clean them, bottoms and tops.

Marissa let out a short pleased "hmph" and pushed each foot into his mouth. He licked and sucked on her bootleather, cleaning the indentations on the bottom with his tongue, swallowing the mud and filth in exaggerated gulps for her benefit.

She spread her legs and patted her belly. Jonah licked upward, moving his face toward the split in her legs, sinking his tongue into her slit. She put her hand on her belly and pulled back, making the entire area more accessible to him.

She leaned over and pulled something from the edge of her desk.

It was a little tattoo gun.

"Jonah, do you want one?"

It had never occurred to him that Marissa could give him a tiny tattoo, but he did get that one at her party.

The pips meant information.

He kept his tongue lodged in her pussy as he looked up to nod.

"Tell me."

"Yes, I want a pip, perfect sir."

Mariss smiled, petting his head. She pushed her pussy into his mouth, letting it sit there as he sucked. She turned around and bent over the desk. He started sucking her ass with abandon, licking and sucking it as though it were the only food in the world.

"Use your hands."

He put his hands on her ass, spreading it open so he could suck and lick deeper. He could hear her moan as his tongue landed in her deepest spaces, trying to burrow its way inside her. She pushed her ass backward and ran her fingers over her clit. He dove in more enthusiastically and ate her ass while she jerked her little button. He slid one hand inside her pussy and pressed backward, letting him get just another quarter fo an inch in. He could feel his own tongue through the wall between her pussy and rectum.

He felt her buck and heard the lower, louder moans that meant she was about to cum. He fastened his lips onto her asshole and held on tightly while she shook her ass in his face, spraying drops of cum over his hands and arms.

She grabbed his wrist and placed the tattoo gun on it, creating a sixth circle next to the one before.

This one was on the bone and it hurt quite a lot, despite being so small. Marissa put the gun down and grabbed his hand. She pulled him into a room next to her office.

As she opened the door, Jonah saw it was a large shower room, with jets everywhere. It was seemingly bult entirely out of grey stone and there were hoses running across the walls. In the center of it was an indent- a sort of hot tub that opened up into the greater shower space.

Marissa pulled her shirt off and threw it out the door, closing it behind her. She stood there in just her boots. Jonah moved to the center of the pool and stepped in, stepping down a few feet. As she stepped over, he could see that his face was, again, at the level of her pussy, as he stood in the indent.

Marissa looked at him and then glanced to her upper right. Jonah snuck a peek in that direction and saw a camera, much like the one in his office. She turned to the pole behind her and pressed a button. Water began spraying down around them everywhere. It seemed like it was coming from all sides. It was cold, pouring down on Jonah, colder than he expected. He looked at the pole and saw it glowing blue. He breathed in, shocked by the temperature, naked, shivering. Marissa was out of the main path of the jets. She stepped around him, watching him. She leaned back on the pole, pushing her hand lower.

He saw the glow change to cyan, powder blue, lighter. And the water became frigid. Jonah closed his eyes and whimpered. He began to lose feeling in his toes as he willed his feet to stay in the indent. The water creeped up his legs, seemingly colder every inch. He let his arms fall to his sides as Marissa picked up a hose. She pointed the hose at him and squeezed the trIgger.

Suddenly a blast of ice cold water shot out at his chest. He growled, shaking, feeling the water slam into him. He was working to stand upright. She sprayed his face until he couldn't feel it anymore.

And still, his hands stayed at his waist.

"Turn around and bend over."

Jonah did, intentionally spreading his ass. All he could think of was Giselle jumping up and stripping her pants off to take a picture of her ass in front of the people she worked with, just to make him happy.

What must they have thought?

She didn't care.

The light behind Jonah's eyes went red as she sprayed the hose directly into his asshole. It was so powerful he could barely stay upright. And the temperature was sub arctic.

He lost feeling in his cock and balls as Marissa sprayed them until, finally, advancing to the side of the indentation and placing the hose nozzle in his anus. He breathed in, terrified, and put his hands on the side of the indent in the floor. As she turned it on, he screamed, breathing hard as the ice cold water shot up inside him.

And then, suddenly, it all disappeared. Heat lamps flashed on as the water poured down open drains. In less than a minute, it was all gone, leaving Jonah panting, water dripping from inside him down the shower drain.

Marissa stood up and stepped back to the pole.

"Jonah, stand up and face me."

"Yes, Sir." He slowly rose to his feet and faced her.

She pressed the pole and it glowed red. The water in the room began to drip down.

It was hot.

She directed the hose at him. "Count to ten in a slow and steady pace."

Jonah began counting as she directed the hose at his cock. The jackhammer stream that hit him between the legs was hot. He started, as slowly and steadily as he could.

"1, 2, 3, 4, 5, 6…"

"Don't speed up. Start again."

He moaned in pain. "Yes, sir. 1,2,3,4,5,6,7,8,9,10"

She let go of the trigger and he slumped over. The pain was intense. Jonah was used to hot showers, but this was at the top end of anything he'd experienced.

She touched the pole at a height over her head and it glowed orange. He started breathing heavily. This would be hotter. How could he deal with that?

The water around him felt ready to boil his skin.

He looked at Marissa's face. She looked almost apologetic as the let loose with the hose.

Jonah felt as though his skin would come off. He screamed, feeling the water beat against him. She pointed the hose between his legs and his prick felt like it was immersed in boiling water. He started to cry.

It took every inch of his willpower not to cover himself, to protect himself with his hands.

And he didn't.

She told him to bend over and spread his ass with his hands.

Jonah begged her. "Please. Please. Please."

But he did it.

She directed the hose at the opening in his ass and let loose a rain of fire that tore him in half. He screamed out, sobbing.

Marissa dropped the hose and reached for the pole. The hot water poured away through the drains as room temperature water filled in the space behind it. Jonah fell into the tub indentation, breathing heavily.

Marissa stepped over and sat on the edge, pulling him to her. She opened her mouth and kissed him.

He eagerly kissed her back, grabbing and holding her, sobbing and running his hands over her.

She held him and calmed him down, petting him as his breathing returned to normal and he sank into her kisses. They kissed over and over and Jonah felt himself feeling almost normal. His skin was raw and red and his throat was torn up from screaming. But he wanted to make Marissa happy.

And she saw that.

She pulled him up to the top of the indent, sitting him down. She sat in his lap, facing him, and wrapped her legs around him, positioning his prick so it could slide up her ass easily.

"Stay there. That's good. This is something you owe me, right?"

"Yes, sir." Jonah's prick was still raw, but it felt good inside her. For a second, his brain tried to tell him that everything good came from Marissa. And Marissa had come from Eve.

Everything good came from Eve.

"You did really good, Jonah. Tonight's going to be hard."

"I know, sir."

"Do you like getting my ass as a reward?"

Jonah tried to just feel. "I really do. It feels so good, sir."

"Why didn't you try to protect yourself?"

"Are you proud of me?"

Marissa grabbed his hair. "Answer my question."

He paused for a minute. "Eve wouldn't like it."

She leaned in and whispered in his ear. "That's a good answer."

She rode him slowly, starting and stopping, enjoying the way he felt. He caressed her face in adoration, kissing her slowly until, finally, she told him it was ok to cum for her, up inside her ass. She placed her hands on Jonah's nipples and twisted them as he came, feeling the pretty warmth of him.

They stayed like that for a while.

"Jonah. I need you to come in here and lick your cum out of my ass, ok?"

He nodded, "yes, sir."

She slid off his still hard shaft and pulled him to a white door at the edge of the shower room. It was a tiny bathroom. He followed her in as she leaned over the sink, letting him drop between her legs. As he started to lick, letting his load dribble out of her, Marissa whispered.

"There are no cameras in here. Things are about to move very quickly. Remember what I said to you about the chess board."

He licked her and listened. Her ass was open and wet and accessible. "Yes, sir."

She turned and grabbed his head. "Jonah, look at me."

He tried to look into her eyes. It was hard to think.

"Jonah. Don't get too attached to this world."

And that's when she said the thing that woke him up completely.

"It's not real."

Chapter 15

5 years ago

Eve walked up to Jonah in the crafts store holding two pieces of fabric. "Excuse me, are you a DJ?"

Jonah cocked his head. For a second, he considered lying. Then, he thought better of it. "No. I'm not a DJ."

She laughed, "Good, because I can't really ever ask a DJ anything anymore."

He looked at her. It was hard to tell what race she was but she was a stunning woman. Her hair was dark, with about 5 different browns mixed in. Her skin was flawless and her eyes were jet black, like black marbles floating in milk. But, despite all that, and a remarkably curvy and beautiful shape, it was her lips that stood out. They looked wet and hypnotically kissable. For a second, Jonah couldn't breathe.

She showed him the two swatches, "Do these two blues match well?"

Jonah inhaled. "Well, first of all, you're right. There is no way a DJ could properly answer this question."

"I figured."

"I would say they aren't the same, but they are nicely complementary. Like far enough away that it doesn't look like YOU think they are the same."

She looked at them. "Ok. I buy that."

"I'm Jonah. I do reds and yellows, too, if you're interested." He reached his hand out. Eve liked his height. They were very close to being the same height. And his face looked like it was good at smiling. Good at being happy. Which sounded silly, in her head. But it was important.

She shook his hand. "Wow. You've got depth. I'm Eve."

He sighed, "not sufficient depth for this task here."

She saw the array of things in his cart. It held molds and forms of varying kinds and sizes.

"Maybe I can return the favor?" Eve winked at him.

At that moment, it became clear to Jonah that he would say or do anything to keep this conversation going. "Ok, I'll tell you my shame over here if you promise to one day tell me the DJ story."

"Ok, but it'll break your heart."

"We are finishing a project at work and I want to make cupcakes for my team to celebrate and I don't know what shape to make them. Not a greek tragedy, but…"

"Oh my god." Eve smiled. Jonah's brain felt like it might leak out of his ears. "There is so much here I need to know."

They started down the aisle slowly. "Ok, I'm a project manager. The project is a mobile data delivery system, which even puts me to sleep. And the flavor profile is like devil's food, I think."

"Well Devil's food data cupcakes sound good." She leaned on his cart.

"Yeah, anything sounds good when YOU say it."

"One to ten, are you a baker?"

Jonah held up ten fingers. "I'm glad you asked. 10. 10 I'm a baker. I can bake the fuck out of these."

"German coconut or cream cheese?" She put her swatches in the top basket of his cart as she walked with him. His heart jumped. That meant she would walk all the way to the counter with him if he played this right.

"The right questions, yes. It depends on the form factor. I love both." He stopped for a second. "And look, clearly you have a far more sophisticated pastry sensibility than my team does."

"Clearly."

"So I will move in whatever direction you think makes sense."

She picked up two of the molds and put one back. "Here. this one. Fit it in this one. Now you can make little cellphones. Chocolate Mobile cupcakes."

He nodded. "That is brilliant. You may have solved all my evening's problems. Do we need to get these cut for you? Sidequest?"

"Yes. this one is little shorts. This one is little top."

He smiled. "I like it. The tinier the outfit, the cheaper."

"That's the idea." She grabbed his arm and pointed him toward the cutting table.

They talked and laughed while the man at the table cut her fabric. Jonah slid the rolls of newly cut fabric into his cart and they explored the store for a bit longer before finally checking out.

By the time they stepped out the door to the parking lot, it was getting dark. Jonah watched Eve move as she slipped the bag over her shoulder.

Was she wasting time?

He grabbed his bag, "Did you want a ride home?"

Eve laughed and put her hand on the crook of his arm. "I was just about to ask the same thing. If you wanted a ride."

"Ah. If you had asked first, I would have just abandoned my car forever." It's possible that he was telling the truth.

"Just like that, huh?"

"I'm a decisive kind of guy. I know I looked a bit lost in there, but..."

"Oh, I think you handled yourself well in the middle of all the choices."

Jonah nodded, "Oh, no doubt, it's a big store."

She leaned in toward him. "You're wasting time now."

He felt how close she was. He could smell her hair. Her lips were less than a foot away from him. "I just shopped with you. And now I want to kiss you. This has never happened with my other shopping buddies."

She smiled. "Can you make it a long one? I could use a long kiss." She moved a few inches closer.

He nodded."I can definitely do that."

And the kiss never stopped.

***

Today

Jonah drove to the location in Marissa's email. It looked like a hotel or a convention center. It was in a part of town he'd never been to. The stairs to the lobby were black marble, heavy and gothic. He stepped in and looked around until he saw a symbol carved into the wall of the lobby. He walked over to it and ran his hand over it. It was a lower case "y" in a circle, stylized exactly as it was at the entrance to Yleros.

And it felt like it had been there for a long time.

He stepped into the glass doors that sat right next to them.

It looked like a bank, with teller areas and tables. It was wide and expansive, seemingly taking up the entire length of the hotel.

He looked around for some entrance, some sign of the event that Marissa expected him to serve. Across the room he saw a familiar person.

Sitting at a desk was the woman from Marissa's Party with the dark red hair. As he approached her he could smell the familiar scent of Lilac. He felt his cock twitch at the memory of her in the bathroom off the hallway that night. There was a wooden block on her desk with her name on it.

Arete Kassal.

Somehow knowing her full name made this harder. She was a real person. He sat down in the chair in front of her desk as she finished what she was writing and looked up at him.

She shook her head. "Jonah, don't look directly at me."

He averted his eyes. "Yes, sir."

"I'm going to take you where you need to go. But first, I need to go over some things with you."

Jonah was confused. He looked around. There were about 12 women here, in this space, each preoccupied with what they were doing.

What was this place?

"My name is Arete Kassal. I am Eve Ungaro's Lawyer. I have prepared these documents for you to sign."

Jonah looked down, more confused than ever, and began reading.

"I can give you an overview if you like? Jonah?

He nodded.

She continued, "These say that you are no longer an autonomous citizen. You are owned by Eve Ungaro.

You give up your rights to own property of any kind, possessions or a bank account and for the rest of your life agree that you will not work and will remain in Ms. Ungaro's possession."

"Holy fuck."

"You can read it yourself. I'll give you a few minutes." She placed a pen on the desk next to him.

"Is this binding?"

She took a breath. "Not here. Here they are mostly ceremonial."

This made Jonah wonder. If not here, then where?

"What happens to the money in my bank account and to what I own?"

Arete stood up and leaned against her desk. "You forfeit them. You give them up. Eve has money."

As she said that, it started to feel real. This wasn't a joke anymore. This wasn't a role play.

"Can I talk to Eve?"

She folded her arms. "Soon. Let me know when you are ready to sign. I'll need you to put your driver's license and wallet here on the desk, along with your clothes.

This was something Jonah had never considered. He tried to steady his breathing.

She kneeled down in front of him. "Jonah, look at me. It's ok. I'm telling you. Look at me. Breathe." She reached for his hand.

"I don't understand."

"Do you remember telling Eve that you wanted her to own you?"

Jonah thought back. He absolutely remembered that. Was all this because of that moment? Was any of this legal?

"What about my car?"

"You forfeit ownership of that. You won't have a driver's license anymore anyway, so it's a nonstarter. You wouldn't be able to drive it. You can leave your keys here, too."

"I'm supposed to serve at this event tonight."

She snapped at him, trying to get him to look straight ahead. "Jonah, listen closely. I will take you where you need to be. Relax. You won't be late. You need to read these and sign, do you understand?"

He put his hands on the desk. "Ok, if I could just talk to Eve."

"You can't. Do you understand?"

Jonah closed his eyes. Out of everything he had done so far, this was far and away the hardest part. He stood up. Without looking around, he began to remove his clothes. Arete Kassal stepped back around to her seat and watched.

He flipped to the last page of the document. There was a space for him to sign. And right next to that was the line with the text "Eve Ungaro" below it.

Below the line where Eve had already signed.

His vision seemed to close in, creating a tunnel in front of him. He stood up.

Before taking his pants off, he removed his wallet and keys. He placed them in a pile next to his neatly folded clothing. He sat down, nude, and lifted the pen.

It felt like it weighed 100 pounds.

Without reading any further, he signed the document on the line at the end over the printed version of his name.

As he signed, he recognized the irony. He wrote out "Jonah Gilden," but upon doing so, he no longer felt like Jonah Gilden. He was just Jonah now, maybe.

He was just property.

Arete Kassal checked off two boxes on a piece of paper, put the paper on top of his items and shuffled them into her desk drawer. From another drawer she pulled out a tattoo gun and pulled his wrist toward her.

Jonah looked up as she placed two pips on his wrist, evenly, lined up with the six already there. She took her time, seemingly making sure that the tiny circles were all equally spaced and perfect. 8 tiny circles altogether.

In the corner of the room, as his eyes scanned the ceiling, he saw another camera. He wondered why he wasn't cold, then realized that the temperature in this space was much higher than he had originally thought. None of the women stared, even as he stood up, Arete holding his arm as she escorted him nude to the bank of elevators behind them.

As he stepped into the elevator, the Lawyer wrapped her arms around him and kissed him. She whispered in his ear, "You're doing really well, Jonah. Please do not freak out."

He kissed her back.

She had said "Please" to him. In the elevator, where there were no cameras.

She said "Please."

***

3 Years ago

Jonah brought the bowl and slid it on the table in front of her. Eve looked down and then back at him. "What's this?"

"I don't want to fight."

"Were we fighting?"

Jonah sat next to her. "You put your shirt on."

Eve laughed. "Sweetheart. Just because I put my boobs away, doesn't mean I'm mad at you."

"Seems like it."

Eve took a bite of the soup. "This is amazing. What is it?"

He smiled. "It's like a Thai coconut soup."

"I don't have anything in my apartment to make this. What did you do?"

Jonah put her feet in his lap. "You had come coconut milk in a can. I made some tofu out of chickpeas. You had lime juice near the alcohol. You know. Stuff."

"You can't make tofu out of chickpeas."

"Yes, you can. And the chickpea juice can be whipped to add texture. It's called Aquafaba."

"You take that back."

"I can't. It's done. I said it."

Eve leaned in and kissed him. "I'm not mad. I'm sorry if I came off that way."

"I'm really sorry I missed the reading. I really wanted to be there. I love your readings. The traffic just crushed me."

Eve ate some more. "I know. I know. Too many people in this city. They all live between you and me."

"Every fucking one of them."

Eve thought for a second. "Did I have cilantro?"

"I stole it from the bag of tacos from lunch."

"Holy Jesus, you are a crazy motherfucker." Eve took a big sip from the bowl. It really was very good soup.

"You can't stop me. You can't hold me back."

Eve looked at him. She pulled her shirt off and tossed it at him.

He grabbed it and smelled it, setting it on the couch behind him. "Thank you. Thank you for freeing the girls."

"This really was good. Unfortunately the soup didn't make it. It died."

"I'm glad."

"I'm sorry I was pissy. I was going to dedicate something to you."

"So everyone would know I was banging you?"

"Yeah. That was actually part of the dedication. Confirming people's suspicions that you were banging me."

"That would have really helped my reputation, you know."

She climbed over him, putting her boobs in his face. "I know. You needed this."

"I did." He kissed her. "Can you do a reading just for me?"

"You went to school, dick, read it for yourself." She sunk into a long kiss, pressing him down into the couch.

"You think just because you can read that everyone can, don't you?"

"I've seen your lips move at the subtitles." She licked his lips and ran her hands over him.

Jonah laughed. "You *were* mad at me."

"I still am, fucker. Don't you want to punish me?"

"I do. My spanking hand is itching." he said, like a cowboy.

"That's weird, don't do cowboy. But spank me."

Jonah rolled over and watched her crawl forward on the couch. She put her head over the arm and stuck her ass in the air. Her hands slid behind her, waiting.

Jonah felt the round curves of her ass through her white velour shorts. From the back, they rode up so high that the perfect globes were clearly visible, poking out from the bottom. He leaned over and kissed her back, holding her arms behind her, Twisting them up with one hand, pressing against the small of her back. She arched her back more, letting the shorts slip a bit more as they threatened to expose the soft and pillowy lips between her legs.

Before the shorts were able to give up completely, Jonah ran his finger under the waistband behind her and pulled them down, letting them snap around her ass and collect at the top of her thighs. He placed his hand behind her, letting it rest over the surface of her soft wet pussy, glistening in the half light of her apartment.

He whispered, "10, and she nodded.

He pulled his right hand back and slammed it into the left hemisphere of her ass. She lifted her bottom and moaned, "1"

Jonah redirected his hand to her other cheek, bringing it down almost vertically, on to the meaty part of her, listening to the slap as it rang throughout the room.

"2"

She slowly spread her legs as he hit her twice in a row, hard, alternating between the cheeks of her ass.

"3, 4" She moaned and slowly rocked as he spanked her three times quickly in succession.

"5, 6, 7."

He pulled back, punching her down into the couch even harder, trying to make her feel taken, Slapping her again and again.

"8,9,10." She turned, pulling him down and spreading her legs. He dragged his hand and placed it at the root of her, over her pussy. He felt the slick wetness, cooing his raw hand. He slowly let it wander over her cunt, exploring, playing with her pretty clit while she let her legs fall to the sides, like a frog, and kissed him on the lips.

She whispered, "Maybe you should move in with me."

He massaged her pussy, digging his face into her neck. "Is that what you want?"

"You can make sure i don't starve and that I get fucked regularly."

"That's sounds like a great fucking job." Jonah said, laughing into her neck.

She wrapped her hands around him, throwing her right leg off the couch, spreading wider for him.

"You already fed me. Maybe it's time to fuck me."

"Will you read to me if I do?"

"I only read to roommates." Eve was breathing harder.

Jonah leaned in, putting his knee between her legs. He'd already decided he wanted to live with her.

So now, let's see how the rest of the night would go.

"

Chapter 16

The elevators opened to a wide open white library, where Jonah was surrounded by women. Arete whispered in his ear.

"Hold it together."

And, looking around, he could see why. The room was filled with women, with one or two men walking around naked, as he was, serving. But that wasn't the amazing thing.

The women were all dressed in random ways, from completely nude women to women in elaborate dresses and suits. There were women of every size and shape,

And seemingly every color.

He saw a woman who was deep dark blue black, with long white hair. He saw two pink women walking together. In front of them, a woman whose skin was bright red. He saw a golden woman, with copper red hair and a greyish woman, beautiful and clay like.

Arete Kassal pulled him over to a table in the corner and picked up a tattoo gun. She lifted his chin. "Your two last ones. Are you ready?"

He nodded. She slowly tattooed two final tiny circles on his wrist.

If he could get 10, there would be answers.

She led him to a mat in the middle of the room with a thin rope around it. A darker man stood on it already. He was nude as well.

Arete let go of his arm.

"You are entertainment. This is Oyelo. And that little sign is your instructions.

Jonah looked over and saw a long sign, below the rope. He guessed people in the audience would press buttons to make symbols appear. As he stepped onto the mat, the first symbol lit up. It showed a man standing while another gave him head.

Jonah stepped over and dropped to his knees, taking the other man's cock into his mouth and sucking it slowly. It wasn't hard yet, but slowly began to fill his mouth thickly. He pushed his head down on it, pulling out to lick the base and shaft and then sliding it back in his mouth.

He closed his eyes and tried not to think of anything. He heard a notification, similar to the one on his phone and the symbol disappeared while the one next to it, showing two men in a 69 position, lit up.

He felt Oyelo slide down to the mat and begin to suck him as well. He had leaned back and pulled the man on top of him so he could access his prick better as a voice came over the PA.

"Ladies. The reason you are here tonight. From her home. Eve Ungaro."

It resonated in Jonah's ears as he sucked on the man, holding him. He couldn't see anything but his cock, in front of him.

Then he heard Eve's voice.

"I am so honored to be here tonight. I'm grateful for the opportunities. But more than that, I'm grateful to the people here who have given me so much."

The room filled with applause as she continued.

"I chose this for tonight. This is a shorter passage from an earlier book in the series. It's called 'The Queen's Burden.'"

She continued

"Once, a very long time ago, the Alitha, the goddess of love and possibility, laid with Meg Paratha, the ancient god of war, to finalize their contract to release the people that Alitha held dear from the constant terrors of war. "

"Meg paratha had agreed to the deal not just because of Alitha's beauty, but because she had agreed to bear him a child that might carry with her some of his dark countenance. Ten years passed as Alitha's belly grew large and she waited to bear his child, ten years so that the child could grow slowly, and, she hoped, be nurtured by her spirit, her ability to love, from within her body."

"The child who was born came to be known as Nadira, the goddess of intimate pains. And she heard the prayers of lovers who had to endure great pain to pursue their love. She was feared by some but widely held in high esteem by the people who, without restraint, worshiped her mother."

"Many, many years later, there was a kingdom with a Queen, named Zoka, who ruled compassionately, with care, and listened to her people. The people cherished her and rallied around her. Alongside her sat, though, the one the people loved more than anything. Her consort, Sahali. He was beautiful and kind and wise and had served the people so well that they cheered just to hear him clear his throat to speak, knowing that what came from his mouth would elevate them, lift them up."

"But, as much as the people loved her consort Sahali, that amount was nothing compared to his own queen's adoration. Daily, her adoration for him was visible in his deference to him, his appreciation, his joy being in his kind presence. "

Jonah listened, trying to let himself be good entertainment as well. The notification went off and he used the opportunity to try to see Eve. But all he could see was the sign and the ring. It showed a man fucking another man who was laying on his back. Oyelo nodded at him and pushed him down on his back. He was strong and his cock was slippery and sleek from Jonah's attention. It ent up his ass quickly and Oyelo began fucking him.

He heard Eve's voice continue.

"For many years, the love between the queen and her consort kept them young. And it spurred the people in their kingdom to seek out their own love, to build it even higher. The kingdom flourished and soon came to the attention of Meg Paratha. "

"The God of War was angry, and he feared that the people in this kingdom felt love so acutely, so intensely, that they didn't fear death. And Meg Paratha wasn't just a blood soaked angry war god. He was a sensible one, as well. A people that did not fear death would hold no fear of war, not fear of loss. A people like that could not sustain themselves. "

"So he called Nadira to his side, Opening wide his lap for his daughter, who sat nestled against him, his giant hand around her lithe waist. "

"He asked his daughter to appeal to Alitha, to create some compromise where the people of this kingdom would know more than just unsullied vanilla-white love. Nadira, filled as well with her mother's spirit, made a deal with him out of love."

"Alitha understood and allowed Nadira to execute her deal. The next morning Nadira appeared to Queen Zoka and her remarkable beloved consort and made a deal."

"Meg Paratha would agree to keep their kingdom safe from war under one condition. A deal to be carried out on the night of the first day of each month. On that day, Queen Zoka would wake up and care for his consort's needs in every way. She would remind him how much she loved him. And then, once it was dark, she would strip him forcefully and beat him with a whip. She would make sure not to spare any of his precious areas but to beat him all over every part that hurt the most. For his part, Sahali would let his hands drop to his side as she accepted the strokes, each one harder than the last. "

Jonah started to feel like Eve had chosen this for him. He wondered if she could see him from where she was reading as he let the man move faster and faster inside him. The notification alerted him to a new symbol, suggesting he turn and bend over

So he did. Oyelo began fucking him harder.

Eve continued, "She would then take him, with no regard for his modesty, to the stage at the center of town. She would roughly take him on the knotty wooden floor of the stage, then call on the people of the town to exercise their own worst desires on his body. The people of the kingdom would come up, many at a time, and make use of his body, their hands free to roam all over him, their eyes free to inspect him, beating him, loving him, in their own way, like animals until morning."

"And the next morning, the Queen would carry him home where the Goddess Nadira would meet them, wiping away his wounds and lingering pain. Sahali the consort would be made like new again and would spend the day in the arms of his queen. "

"It was through this routine that the people learned about pain, about hurt. They learned to fear, even as they learned to incite pain. But the next day, the queen's unwavering adoration for her consort reminded them that pain is not the end. That all hurt ends and leaves only love behind."

"The sullen god of war was appeased and his daughter, Nadira, grew in favor and visage with the people until they found her as beautiful as they did her mother. The people recognized the role of pain and loss in love. "

"To this day, Nadira claims priests and priestesses who serve her quirks, in love, delivering pain of a certain kind to lovers, reminding them that love endures."

The darker man came hard inside him as the room erupted in cheers and applause. Jonah let himself fall over on his back, laying there, the other man next to him, as his breathing returned to normal and no more notifications came.

And that's where he stayed until Arete stepped over, now nearly nude, and helped him up. She led him to a doorway at the edge of the space and adjusted his hair.

She looked into his eyes, "Hey, Jonah. Are you ok?"

He looked at her and burst out in tears. She held his head and rocked him. "Yeah. I'm ok. I'm so confused."

She held him closely. "It's time for answers, right?"

He nodded, still crying.

She held his head and wiped his tears. "Hey. I want to have the chance to get to know you better. I think you're amazing."

He nodded slowly. She opened the door and he half expected to see Eve.

It wasn't her.

Jonah stepped into the room. It was lean and white and open, surrounded by windows, with one wall of plants falling from the ceiling downward. It was beautiful, really. In the center of it was a woman. She was tall and lithe and had long black hair with a bright red streak in it. She wore a pretty white dress, open in front, exposing most of her skin.

Sin that was a dark, deep maroon, from head to toe.

It was a color no person from earth could ever possibly be.

She stepped forward and took his hand, pulling him to a wide white couch where she sat down, crossing her legs.

Jonah knelt down in front of it, staring.

"Are you a history buff, Jonah Gilden. It's ok, you can talk freely to me." her voice was smooth as he realized there was no way of telling how old she was.

He nodded, "I am."

She smiled. "Good. From what I've seen of you, you seem capable of opening your mind quite a lot. I'm going to need you to do that, if you can."

"Thank you." He smiled at her in wonder.

She put her hand down. "I'm Zelea Nova. Can you come sit next to me?"

He stood up and sat on the couch, crossing his legs like she had and looking at her. "Sounds like a rock star name."

"It does, doesn't it? I like that." She held his hand. "About 70,000 years ago, a number of different groups of people - of us - were about to step into a war that would have decimated us - reducing the population of the world by 90%. And, in the first salvo, the ones to die? Babies, the infirm, seniors, people who needed help."

Her hand felt perfectly human. Her voice, her aspect. Everything about her except that fascinating color. "That sounds terrible," he responded.

She nodded, "It was. So, all over the world, women rose up and took control from men. Some through subtlety, some through dialogue. Some in horrible ways. But, no matter what the means, by morning, women ruled the world. And within a week, war was unthinkable. Within a month, all weapons that could lead to war were destroyed. Within a year, means were developed to nurture everyone so that no one would want for anything."

"And would have no reason to fight?" He asked.

She continued. "Exactly. You understand. Men were taken care of. They had their place, just not in positions where they could cause damage. Where they could uproot what we were building. Different people merged together in unity. Differences in color became inconsequential. By now you've noticed that our people come in more colors than you've seen here." She played with his hand, rolling it around in hers. She seemed so playful in her mannerisms. Her eyes were dark black, like Eve's.

"I have. If I can ask, what are you?"

"Me? I'm a human, like you. All of us are. Just humans. Well. Within the next 20,000 years, we had built a technologically advanced civilization. Logistics were met with environmentally sound teleportation. Medical issues were met with organic technology that virtually eliminated infirmity and disease. Our food manufacturing and storage became so significantly advanced that the planet could have shut down for a hundred years and still fed all its people every day. "

He squeezed her hand. "That is amazing."

"It was." She leaned in to him and he realized that she smelled woody and good. He recognized the teakwood scent he had smelled on the pink woman before.

"When we began using our science to procreate, we adjusted the population. Men became 10% of the population. That concentration seemed ideal for their participation. We developed medications like Twillerex and Sybo, meant to make sexual interaction completely safe. And then experienced a sexual Renaissance. "

He cocked his head. "How so?"

She smiled. Jonah decided that she was openly sexy. In a way few regular people are. She seemed constantly flirtatious, even when telling some alternate universe history. "With men dramatically in the minority and women freed from fear, from responsibilities around sexual safety, women became sexually awakened. They reveled in the joy of a sexuality they could leverage at their discretion, any way they liked. Social boundaries around sexuality fell while physical ones toppled. The remaining men worked hard to be safe. " She lit up. "Our world became liberated." She breathed out. "But there was a price to be paid. The leadership of the world didn't consider it a trivial thing that to achieve our happiness we had subjugated all men. We wished there was another way. "

Jonah looked down. "I understand that."

She brushed a hair out of Jonah's face and he suddenly realized how naked he was. She looked down to see his erection. "I'm sure you do, Jonah. So we built ten experimental planets. It took us 5,000 years, but we did it. We populated them with people and gave them choices on how to build their cultures. We helped them write backstories and forge histories so that none of them would know their planets weren't young."

He nodded, breathing out slowly, "And not real."

She tipped her head sympathetically. "Yes. And not real. Bako became a planet where people were culturally commanded to have sex only once for each partner. Archon became a mirror of Yleros, a place where men were powerfully and sometimes cruelly in charge."

She took a deep breath. "And Earth. A place where men were nominally in charge and sexually repressed."

He stared at her. "Earth?"

"And 7 more planets, each in different solar systems, with different properties, habitable by humanity."

He repeated. "Earth is an experiment?"

She nodded and held both his hands. "Yes, just as all of them are. 20,000 years ago, they were finished and set spinning. And we monitored them, from our ancestral planet- from our home."

Jonah tried to process it all. "What was the main planet- the real one."

"I thought you would have figured it out. It was Yleros. That's the real home of humanity. "

He closed his eyes and dropped his head. "Oh my god."

She put her hand under his chin and lifted his head. "Are you ok?"

"I am. This is just..."

She stood up and stood in front of him. "I know. Come here. " She pulled his legs apart from his cross legged pose, pulling her dress open completely in front and sliding on top of him.

His cock slid easily into her as she sat down all the way, putting one foot on either side of the sofa beside him and pulling him closer. He felt her slick pussy envelope him.

"Wow."

She kissed him. "Is that better? We watched the experiments. We don't know why the only way humanity flourishes and grows kind, survives in joy, is with women in charge. We have no idea. But none of the experiments were places you'd want to live."

He was rocking back and forth slowly inside her. She was warm and soft, her belly pressed against his. "Not even Earth?"

She smiled as she fucked him slowly. "What do you think?"

He laughed a tiny laugh. It was all so surreal. "You aren't wrong."

"Two years ago, we identified an asteroid headed toward Earth. It would be too small to damage an ordinary planet. But for one built as an experiment?"

His breathing was faster. He whispered. "It will wipe us out. "

She whispered back, "Yes." She moved back and forth smoothly. "We built a network to test the men who might want to come home to Yleros. Women are welcome, of course. The other experimental planets did the same." Grabbing his arm, she kissed her tattoos. "Your invitation was dependent on these."

He looked over. "The tattoos."

She planted tiny kisses all over his face as she rode him. "And how you received them. We've watched. We've watched you remain kind and nonviolent as you've endured significant abuse and degradation. And you've done it without lifting your hand."

Jonah felt himself begin to cum. He was holding off as long as he could. Zelea's cunt began to contract over him, dripping onto his lap. She was cumming. She kissed his hand. That was the last straw for him. She put her hands behind his neck and whispered. "Ooh, that feels nice. Thank you."

He came in long waves, holding her tightly, feeling her weight on him. "Thank you. That was great. And thank you for..."

"For informing you?" She said, biting his ear.

"I guess." He realized he was so starved for information that he was experiencing deep feelings. And Arete, who had been kind to him, there, at the end. So much was falling into place.

She rocked back and forth in a relaxed way in his lap, running her hands over him. "She's in the other room waiting for you. She loves you very much, you know. "

He bent his head down and kissed her breast. The tip of it was so dark red it was nearly black. "I love her."

She stood up slowly, letting her white dress flow around her. "I know. I watched you sign away everything. I saw you give up everything."

Jonah tried to figure out what to say. His mind was racing. "The earth will be destroyed?"

She stepped over to a bar he hadn't noticed and grabbed two glasses, bringing one for him. It was orange juice. This was the first time at one of these events that a woman had handed him a drink. It felt so strange.

She took a sip and sat down again. "Yes. And you would be welcome in at least 5 of the other experimental worlds. You'd be welcome at Archon. It's a cruel place, but you would be a leader, very nearly a god. With power over every beautiful woman you saw. "

He drank looking at her over the rim of the squat glass. "But they aren't real?"

She shook her head. "They are as real as Earth."

Standing back up, she motioned to him to get up as well. "But, come on." She kissed him lightly, whispering, "Don't keep her waiting."

***

Eve was standing in the other room in her white top and shorts. Jonah didn't realize until that moment how badly he needed to see her. He stepped forward and hugged her.

She ran her hands through his hair. "Jonah."

He let out a long sigh. "This is insane."

She kissed his neck. "I know the last 24 hours have been a handful. "

He pulled back and looked at her. "First, though. A long time ago, you told me I could read for myself. I just wanted you to know that it's nothing like hearing you read."

She smiled. "Really?"

He held her hands. "That was so beautiful. It always is. But tonight was even…"

Eve looked at him, her black eyes digging deeply into him. "Thank you." She pulled him over to the window. "Do you have any questions?"

Jonah put a hand on the window and looked out. The city really was beautiful. "I think I understand it all."

Eve leaned against the wall. "There are no more cameras. It's just you and me. No more tests." She lowered her voice. " No more lies."

He continued to stare. He realized now why the city had felt so empty lately. Because it was. People were leaving. Disappearing to different worlds. "I get that you couldn't tell me everything." He looked at her and smiled. "But I do keep thinking about stuff I left in my car."

Eve laughed. "Oh, god, I never liked your car."

"Well." he steadied himself against the window. "That's something you could have told me before I gave it away."

"What was it you said about your old apartment when you moved in with me?" Eve moved closer until her lips were right in his face.

"Oh, that old thing…"

She reached between his legs and felt the slickness of his cock. She put her fingers in her mouth, tasting Zelea and closing her eyes. "I loved it when you did that. You were so strong. You were like, I don't need to have this apartment to be Jonah. You walked away from it and you were the exact same person."

He spread his legs and leaned into her. "In a little bigger kitchen."

She looked wistful. "You have choices to make."

Jonah nodded, "I know." He ran his hands through her hair and stared at her. "I just realized. Your skin tone…"

"Yeah. I've spent time on Yleros. The suns there do different things. It brings out a red in me. "

He shook his head. How much had he missed. How behind was he? "I see that now. "

"Look," She grabbed his ass and pulled him close, kissing him. "I'm going to be here for a good part of the night, getting stuff packed up, making sure we aren't forgetting anything. Why don't you go home. And rest and think. There are clothes for you in the closet and money for a cab." She pointed to the table next to her.

He kissed her back. "I might walk around a bit."

Eve smiled. "I know where to find you."

Chapter 17

Jonah sat at the edge of the pool a few blocks from his place. It's funny how he had stopped thinking of it as Eve's place and then, now that he was leaving his job, he started calling it that again.

Eve's place.

He pulled his shirt off and threw it in. No one was around to enforce any of the rules written on a sign on the wall behind him. It seemed that no matter where he went there were rules on signs on walls. He saw a dark shape next to him. It was Giselle, pulling off her shirt and tossing it to join his. She had a good arm.

She plopped down topless next to him. "Hey"

Jonah had to admit, he felt better with her sitting there. "Hey, yourself."

She pulled her skirt up, exposing herself. Beneath her pink and shaved cunt were 10 diamonds tattooed in a row across her inner thigh. "Look what I got."

Jonah touched them. "Why? Why would you do that?" He considered what he was told about Archon. A cruel and failed place.

She raised the back of her skirt so that her bare ass was on the concrete. "I'm approved. If you want to go to Archon, I can go with you."

Jonah turned to her. "You would do that? You wouldn't go with Eve?"

She put her hand on his. "I love Eve. But if you went there, you would need me." She raised his hand to her mouth and kissed it.

He stared at her. "You would give up everything because I would need you?"

"Yes." She nodded.

He started listing on his fingers. "You could never own anything. You could never practice medicine. It would be..."

She whispered. "It would be my choice."

Jonah shook his head and kicked the water. "I was going to say a big waste."

It was the middle of the day in a public pool. But no one was around. And Jonah now knew why. People were leaving. They were going...

Elsewhere. They were going to Yleros, some of them. The rest to other experimental worlds. Some in crisis.

Giselle stood up and pulled her skirt off, throwing it in, too. She pulled off her socks and shoes, tossing them in, leaving herself completely naked.

"You know, when you play with me, I know you think it's hot to talk about how my pussy is so big."

"I'm sorry...You seemed to respond to it."

She slid back down next to him. "Oh, I do. It's hot. I'm a tiny girl but I can fit like anything inside me. When you draw lines in marker showing how far things go, I mean, that's so hot. I try not to wash them off."

He nodded. "I noticed that."

Giselle took a deep breath. "When I was young, the doctors told me that I don't have any female reproductive organs in me."

"Giselle Barbier, I didn't know that."

"I don't talk about it. But on the inside, I'm not recognizably female, I guess." She made an apologetic motion with her hand.

"How do you feel about that?"

She rocked on the side of the pool. "Now? at this age? I feel great. I'm like a circus trick."

He rubbed up against her. "A really hot one."

She lifted herself up and slowly slid into the pool. "Exactly. I weigh like 110 pounds and I can fit things in me that weigh that. It's crazy."

"But when you were younger?" Jonah asked.

She treaded water. "I rejected the idea that I'd never be a 'real woman.'"I got super femme. I dressed all girly. I even got extra slutty, which I enjoyed, and still do."

"You are good at it." He smiled.

"You should get in the pool and chokefuck me to prove it."

He smiled and splashed her.

"I dated a guy in med school who said just that. 'A waste.' when I told him. He was trying to be funny. Like 'you're so pretty, what a waste you can't pass those genes on.' He wanted children, too. Bio ones. It was just a joke, I guess."

Jonah shook his head. "But it didn't feel that way?"

"Nope." She spit water at Jonah, who made a big deal out of trying to catch it in his mouth. "I'm comfortable with who I am. I'm a woman. No matter who says what. I'm a doctor. No matter what. And if one of the men on that planet sticks their dick in a toaster at a party, they'll be glad of it. "

He splashed her back. "They will."

She swam slowly over to him and leaned on the edge next to him. "If you go to Archon, I'll come with you."

He petted her head. "I couldn't do that to you."

"I can take a lot more abuse than you think." She winked. She started kissing his leg. "Eve is famous on Yleros. Did you know that?"

Jonah breathed in. "I was starting to see that."

"I think she's afraid to tell you. She's revered. "

Jonah looked over at her. "Do you want to go there?"

She leaned back and let her hair fall into the pool. She laid on her back in front of him. "It sounds amazing. Women can be anything they want. The technology, the civilization. No one needs to work to survive. It's a paradise. And if we were there together, I could still submit to you in private."

He ran his fingers over her chest in front of him. She stuck her nipples out. Her breasts were small enough that they looked nearly flat to her chest like this. He twisted them and she breathed in sharply. He twisted harder. "Yeah? Can I ask you a question?"

She floated closing her eyes in a moan. "Yes."

He twisted harder. "Did Eve send you?"

Her breathing seemed labored as he responded. "No. She knows I'm here. She helped me get the last pip so I could go to Archon."

He let go of one nipple and reached down, grabbing her clit. He started twisting it hard. She moved her legs apart so he could access the little button more easily. "Why would she do that?"

"Because this way, all three of us have a choice, sir." Her belly shook. Jonah could tell how much she was loving this. He twisted even harder, watching her arms and legs open wider.

He lifted slightly, amplifying the pain. "I don't know if I'm built to be…"

"Don't say that sir. That's what Paul said to Grey. He wasn't built for Yleros. To be owned, taken care of. All of it. " Her moaning had increased.

Jonah twisted harder then let go. She sank under for a moment then popped back up, kissing his leg over and over in gratitude.

Jonah looked at her. "He went to Archon? "

She caressed him lovingly. "He did, my sir. Before I was even approved. I didn't have the choice. He didn't want me there. Or Grey."

He kissed her head. "So now what do I do?"

She looked at him confused. "You choose."

Not for the first time, Jonah wondered if Giselle was a bigger or a smaller thinker than he was. He finally decided that it wasn't about that. She was just a wonder.

She was just Giselle.

A shadow fell over him. He looked up and saw Eve.

She smiled at him and crouched down. "Look at this? It's empty. Almost. No rules, huh?"

Giselle pointed up. The meteor would take months to get there. But it was clear in the sky. Tiny but clear.

She said , "That's even kind of pretty. If I squint, I can see it."

Eve agreed. "In a way, it's beautiful, actually."

Jonah leaned in to her. "You helped her get the last diamond?"

She nodded and tousled his hair. "I did. Everyone gets a choice."

"You want her with you, though?"

Eve sat next to him. He saw she was wearing only a Jersey. It was hard not to imagine what she had on under it.

She grabbed his hand. "Of course I do. I've been training her. Just like I've been training you."

Jonah laughed. "Oh, yeah?" He splashed Giselle again and whispered to her. "Where do you go when you go to work?"

Eve smiled and put his hand between her legs. She wasn't wearing anything under it. "Ah. You really know me. I go to Yleros. I have a house there. It's beautiful. There are private spaces for you. I decorated them in ways that I know you'll like. When I'm there, I get your favorite foods and then they go bad and I throw them out because you're not there to cook them. I stole some of your clothes and I keep them in my office so I can smell them when I write."

Jonah kissed her. "I have a drawer in my office of your stuff I can smell." He remembered the letter. How Marissa had given it to HR. "Or I had. I don't know how to be away from you. But I don't know how to do this, either."

She played with his hair, rubbing his hand between her legs. "I told you I'd been training you. For this. To show you that there is more out there for you if you couldn't be with me. And that you could be with me completely." She kissed him. " If you chose it."

"I know that there are no other choices for you."

She kissed his hand. "I'm sorry, no. I'm moving permanently to Yleros soon."

"Well. At least it's not tomorrow. " He pulled her hand closer.

Eve stared him in the eyes. "I love you, you know."

Jonah sighed. "I know. I love you, too. I just may need to go somewhere to think."

She placed a business card sized black envelope on the ground near him. It had a silver "B" on it. "Here."

Jonah picked it up. There was a key in it. "What is this?"

"It's a place to think. And see some other perspectives, maybe." Eve stood up, pointing to where Giselle was pretending to dreown herself in the pool. "I think you should go chokefuck her first."

He reached up and put his hand on her thigh. It was wet and sweaty in the heat.

"Oh, and Jonah. You don't have to come home tonight, but if you do, I'm turning the heat up all the way."

She turned and walked away.

Jonah could feel her sweat on his palm. He closed his hand and held it.

***

He played with Giselle in the pool for a couple of hours until the sun dipped, dropping her off at home fairly battered. She had red marks on her neck, marks that made it fairly obvious what had happened.

He liked the way she begged for it.

He threw on a black shirt and a pair of pants and called a cab to Bako. If he weren't with Eve, he might not have known any of this. He might not have gone anywhere. He wouldn't have these tattoos on his wrist.

He would be in the dark.

People were only allowed to enter individually at Bako. There was a naked woman in front who avoided eye contact. She had short faded blue hair and tattoos around her neck and chest. She was beautiful, with full blue-painted lips and seductive eyes, round and thick breasts, and a chain around her pretty belly. She pointed to the sign which held one word- the one rule they had.

1.   *Once.*

Apparently you couldn't play with the same person twice there. They had cameras everywhere.

It was their only rule.

The woman rolled up his sleeve to see nothing on his upper arm. She smiled at him and grabbed him between the legs as she tattooed an "x" on his upper arm- small enough it was nearly invisible.

He looked at it and nodded.

She sat on the table and swung around, grabbing him with her legs. Faster than he could feel it she had unbuckled his belt and pulled his pants down, docking his prick inside her wet and eager opening.

Jonah didn't know what to do. She smiled at him and kissed his chest, pulling him in and out of her. She was fascinated by the idea that he had no previous tattoos there.

He had never been here.

He looked at the sign. He would have one time with her. Her eagerness was incredibly hot. Having someone just jump him like that was hypnotic. Jonah leaned in and felt his cock movie in and out of her warm cunt, with her staring in his eyes, trying to devour him.

For a moment, he was overwhelmed by the idea that he would never again be able to have this woman. This was a one time only event. He lifted her head and kissed her deeply. She moaned and pulled him inside her, grabbing his ass. He wondered what her voice sounded like, who she was, what her name was. She rubbed her clit, cumming against him as she slapped her pussy into his midsection again and again.

He tried to take her in with his eyes, his senses, to make a permanent memory of this temporary person. She pulled him out as she came and turned over, putting one leg up on the table. Grabbing for Jonah's prick, deftly inserted it into her ass. Jonah tried to enter slowly, but she seemed overwhelmed by the feeling of having a strange man in her ass. She reached back and spread her cheeks, keeping one leg bent on the table.

 A man or two came in behind him. The woman got even more fiercely loud. She yelled out as he came inside her. She lay there for a moment while two men lined up behind Jonah. She pushed him out, fastening a thin clear bracelet to him as he left, and motioned to the man behind him.

Jonah pulled up his pants and stepped past the main door, looking down at the bracelet.

Bako was a kind of madhouse of movement and fetish. A row of men and women were bent over in various poses. Attached to devices that offered up their holes to anyone who passed by. He could see both sides of gloryholes and black rubber coated beds where people chose masked partners. He walked by these and the bracelet glowed green as he passed each.

All the people he had not yet had sex with.

Each time his bracelet glowed green, he attracted the attention of some man or woman. He walked past one of the black beds with a sturdy looking black man on it, partially masked. His cock was pretty and at attention. Jonah stopped by the bed and looked down while the man crawled over to him. For a second, Jonah wondered what the protocol was.

It turned out there wasn't any.

The man reached for his pants and Looked at Jonah in the eye. Jonah laughed and nodded while the man enthusiastically pulled down his pants and pulled him onto the bed with him.

Jonah let his pants come off as he slid the man's cock into his mouth. It was cool and sleek and the head of it seemed enormous, just small enough to make it in his mouth. The man played with his cock, but Jonah wasn't quite ready yet. He turned on his belly and sucked harder, licking the man's balls and the place under them, too.

The man leaned over and grabbed Jonah's ass. Feeling his thick forceful hands there, Jonah spread his legs and arched his back. The man fucked his face harder, having decided that Jonah was a bottom.

He flipped him around, dragging Jonah until his ass was pointed at him. He bent over, licking his ask and warming it up as Jonah stuck it in the air. His cock was sliding into Jonah's ass less than 4 minutes after they had seen each other.

Despite that, the man moved in and out of him slowly, seductively. He moaned with each stroke, seemingly enjoying Jonah, who tried to relax and feel every bit of it. The truth is that he hadn't really considered men as real sex partners until the last couple of weeks. This was the first time he had chosen a man himself to fuck. It felt like a huge event.

And he wished Eve were here.

He thought about her and he pushed backward, fucking the man's cock in a rhythm that felt amazing. He liked the way his hands felt on him. Roaming, almost desperate. And he liked the way people stared. A woman on another bed was being fucked by a larger man, staring at him and biting her lip. He put his head down. If he made a big dramatic deal out of this would he be turning people on? He let go and fucked the cock behind him, yelling out loudly. It all seems simple and performative and ebay for him.

But something about it is so hot.

The man came inside him and he turned around, kissing him on his thick lips. He grabbed his ass and thanked him before standing up to put his pants back on. He almost fell over over.

He looked down.

His bracelet was now red.

Standing up, he walked down the aisle and his bracelet began to glow green again. Every person he passed was new.

There are so many people in the world. So many new people.

He let his cock loll out of the open zipper of his black pants. He could feel it starting to get hard again. He stepped past a table where a tall woman in a full mask sat, legs spread, in a tiny pair of underwear.

Jonah could see she had black x's all over one arm. As he approached, he was able to gauge her height. She might have been nearly 7 feet tall. He moved closer and showed her his bracelet. It glowed green.

Just like hers did.

She motioned him closer and pulled one side of her panties over, revealing a perfectly sleek shaved cunt. Jonah pulled at his cock once or twice until it was nearly hard. She dragged him close and slowly slid it inside her.

By the time he was all the way in, he was rock hard.

He wrapped his arms around her and leaned in. She spoke softly behind the mask.

"My name is Minnete."

"Hi. I'm Jonah."

"Your cock feels really good, Jonah."

He smiled and ran his hands over her naked breasts. They were aerodynamic, as though she were a swimmer.

"Your pussy is amazing. And you are the tallest girl I've ever been inside."

She laughed. "I am really tall. Thank god for this table."

"I know." Jonah kissed the nipple in front of him. "I'd look dumb as hell without it."

"I like how you kiss my tits."

"I'm glad you're here."

"So am I. I hope you get glad inside me."

Now Jonah laughed. "There is no doubt about that. Big secret, I am thinking about baseball really hard."

She pulled him into her and bucked her hips harder, whispering. "Fuck baseball."

"I know. It's not working, anyway."

"It's ok, Jonah. You're the first person to fill me up tonight."

Something about her admission made it nearly impossible to hold back.

Jonah grabbed onto her tits hard and pumped into her slippery pussy until he came.

And then some more.

She reached down and kissed his hand, like Eve had done. He pulled out and she slid her panties back over, "I wish we could make out a little, but I don't want to show my face."

Jonah kissed her nipples and made his way to the door. He stepped outside and sat on the curb, adjusting his pants.

There was no chance, really, that he would ever see Minette again. He considered that for a minute. It felt like a massive powerful loss for some reason.

But it wasn't.

What was he so afraid of letting go of?

What would happen if he never saw Earth again?

The same thing that would happen if he never saw Minette again.

Nothing. He stood up and walked away from Bako and called a cab.

It was dark when he opened the door back home. But the first thing he felt was a tsunami wave of heat.

It was 80 degrees.

He smiled.

Both women were asleep in the bedroom, naked. Giselle had her legs thrown over Eve's belly. Eve's legs were spread widely apart, open in the heat.

Jonah pulled his clothes off and slid into the bed, anxious to avoid waking them up. He laid his face down between Eve's legs, her sweat and juices leaving his cheek slick and wet. He kissed her twice on her lower lips and fell asleep in minutes in his spot.

Chapter 18

There are just about 2,000 stars ranging up to 50 light-years from the Solar System. A little over 60 of them are yellow-orange "G"-type stars similar to Sol - the sun we see from Earth. As many as 15% of them could have Earth-sized planets in the habitable zones.

In 2013, 30 some years ago, astronomers found that, based on Kepler space mission data, there could be as many as 40 billion Earth-sized planets orbiting in the habitable zones of Sun-like stars and red dwarf stars within the Milky Way galaxy.

Eleven billion of these estimated planets may be orbiting Sun-like stars. Many more are circling binary systems, or systems even stranger than that. The nearest such planet was then as close as 12 light-years away but is now estimated slightly above four light-years away.

But there are potentially hundreds of billions of habitable planets out there.

Not all of them are real.

***

Jonah woke up to Eve petting his head. The room was hot and he could feel her sweat and more all over him. Her whole body was glistening, making it look like she'd been oiled down.

He told her and Giselle about his night at Bako.

The three of them touched and kissed. He didn't hold anything back.

"Ok, so what did you find hot about that guy?"

Jonah considered. "I don't know. I've been thinking about that. I never just chose a guy before. I never actively decided to be with one. But he seemed to want me. "

Eve pulled him closer and kissed him deeply. "Of course he did."

She reached down and held his wrist, running her thumb over the row of pips on the inside.

10 of them. Jonah could see her counting, making sure, over and over again.

He stared at her, catching her perfect lips counting under her breath. He wanted to close his eyes to breathe her in but he realized he could never close his eyes while looking directly at her.

It was impossible.

"I'm coming with you."

Eve's eyes filled up and she let out a long sobbing breath. She pulled his wrist to her and kissed it. She kissed it ten times.

Had she been holding her breath?

Giselle kissed his shoulder.

Eve rolled over, sliding on top of him. He felt her sweat everywhere. She fit into him like a jigsaw puzzle just falling into place. His cock slipped without pressure or intentionality inside her perfect pussy. It felt accidental. It felt just like how things worked.

She whispered. "I can never marry you. You would be owned."

He nodded. "I know. I know it all. I'm coming."

She leaned down into his ear. "You can never come back."

Jonah leaned his head over and kissed Giselle. "Doctor, Do you think we've done everything there is to do on Earth?"

She smiled and wrapped her arms around them. "I think we fucking used this place UP."

Eve laughed, sliding against him slowly, their sweat slick and smooth between them. She put her arm around Giselle and moved her hips in a slight circle. He felt her weight on him and it was comforting, liberating.

Jonah always felt strong when she was on top of him. He was the stable surface. He was the rock. He could support her, lift her up. Her weight was slight, but it made him feel like a lifter, like a crane, something made to change things, to move things. He still had so much control and arching his back would let him pull back and push forward. He could press on her back and drive himself deeply into her. He could make her bounce.

And her clit slammed into the area right above his cock, letting him participate in her wet sloppy orgasm, doing his best to be the recipient of all of it.

There is something that happens sometimes when you make a decision. Suddenly, the world conspires to validate it. Like when you choose between the strawberry and coffee ice cream and despite the cost, decide to buy them both, then, later, open up the freezer after you forgot they were both in there.

That was a good call.

In his mind, all the reasons he wanted to come with her swirled around him. And try as hard as he could, he couldn't conjure the reasons not to.

He couldn't manufacture any. And as he came in her, kissing her, none came to mind,

Traveling back and forth between worlds was not cheap or even something that people wanted to do constantly. Subtle adjustments in the portals needed to happen to account for weights and planetary positions.

Eve Ungaro was a mildly well known underground writer here on message boards and BDSM fan sites, writing under the name "Jocasta." Jonah had found and read, he thought, nearly everything she had ever written.

But on Yleros, she was a celebrated Author with a massive following. She was revered. Her writing had taken the age old mythology of Yleros and turned it all into a vibrant modern narrative that captured the zeitgeist all around her. Her trips back and forth to Yleros were commonplace. She read to large groups, appeared in media, interviews, etc.

Eventually she became a part of the culture there.

And she had videos.

The three of them sat in the living room, watching the screen on the wall as they played. Jonah slid in on the floor while the two women sat on the couch. He laughed, recalling why he loved being down here, turning to kiss Eve between the legs.

"I think we'll pretend the shower is broken today, what do you think?"

Jonah smiled, rubbing his face in her. He remembered the beginning of their relationship after he had gotten comfortable enough with their sexual dynamic to politely ask that she maybe not shower before he came over. And how she would meet him at the door, joking about how the shower was broken, tracking his fascination at her smell, her perfect smell.

The screen lit up in the dark room. Eve was on it, wearing a see-through shirt and a tiny skirt.

"Ok. This is on. This is Eve and the amazing tour."

She moved the camera awkwardly and he could see a large modern looking house, covered in glass and ivy behind her. It was seemingly in the middle of a supple looking forest, bright red flowers and purple plants mixed in with the greens.

"This is our house. It seems weird to call it that when you haven't seen it yet. But it's for us. It's where you and me and the doctor woman are going to live. She'll be there to make sure we're healthy. Because who knows. "

She went on. "And here is the pool and the lake right next to it. They both have water in them, but one is big as fuck and the other one has a diving board. You figure out which is which, no hand holding here. Although we can literally hold hands."

She moved the camera toward the side of the house while Giselle laughed. "This is the garden that is my finest accomplishment in the universe, no lie. I've never been able to make anything grow like this on earth. Follow me here."

She focused on individual plants. "These are my heirloom tomatoes. They are every color. They are beautiful. Remember tomatoes. Now, this is my basil and tarragon. I have rosemary here. A lot of it. It's like all of Rosemary. Everyone named Rosemary. And check this out. Eggplants. All purple and beautiful. Eggplants. "

She turned the camera to her face.

"That is a full parmigiana. It's a whole Eggplant Parmigiana garden. That's amazing. If I could grow breadcrumbs it would be complete. You know you want this, Jonah."

Jonah had never seen her look or act this happy, this carefree. He had never seen her giddy like this. Suddenly he felt a wave of sadness.

Had he been holding her back from being truly happy?

He leaned back onto her lap. She whispered, "Ooh, watch this part."

On the screen, he saw her point the camera at the sky. This is where everything became powerfully solid to him. Above her, in focus on the camera, were two suns. One was large and yellow, in the center of the sky, while the other was smaller, more compact. A blue sun slightly below the yellow one. And still, visible in the say, three smaller moons, each barely in view, one with a sharp array of rings around it.

It was real.

She moved into the house, which was beautiful. But all of it was secondary to that single shot of the sky.

He was going to live on another world.

***

Jonah took a shower, to wipe away the sheen of the night before. He was glad he went, for sure, but it would take time to process how he felt otherwise. He was quick, making sure to reinforce the idea that Eve should not think about showering.

Not even a little.

He stepped out of the shower to see all the lights were still off. He realized that Eve and Giselle had packed most everything over the last few days. He caught them merging their bags in the bedroom, noting that there were candles lit everywhere.

"What are you guys up to?"

Giselle had been crying. "We weren't sure if we would be together so we packed separately. I'm basically throwing stuff away."

Jonah came up to her and kissed her eyes, trying to wipe her tears away. "Are you happy?"

"I'm so happy. I'm going to find ways to make sure you are, too."

Jonah nodded at her. "I am happy."

"I wanted to give you this." She handed him a small men's ring.

"Thank you." Jonah took it, looking over at Eve. She nodded at him. He looked at it and slid it on. "What is it for?"

"I know that you belong to Eve. I know she owns you. And that makes me happy. Happy that she has this amazing person. Happy that you get to be owned by someone amazing. But this is from me. It says that you own me. And even though we won't be able to show that in public"

She held it up. "I thought you could touch it whenever you wanted to be reminded that you own me."

Jonah looked at the ring. It was simple. But it was lovely. He asked Eve, "Is this something I can have?"

She walked over and kissed him. "Yes, essentially. In Yleros, men can't own anything. The only things you can have that you can say are yours are things on your body. A piece of Jewelry can be yours. And no one will know in public but when you touch it she will know that you own her - that you're happy to own her." Eve took his wrist. "This is you, giving up everything to be with me." She reached down and touched the pips on Giselle's inner thigh "And this is her, ready to give up everything for you."

She pulled him close and wrapped her hand around his hand that wore the ring. "You hold onto this. It means a lot."

Jonah pulled Giselle into the huddle with him and Eve and wrapped his arms around her. Balancing their public and private lives would take some time to get used to. He kissed her, pushing her down on the floor. Giselle was soft and always responsive. All you ever needed to do was to push a little in any direction and she would move. It's like she was automated, waiting for the chance to comply with a request, no matter how subtle.

She opened her legs and wrapped them around him, putting her arms on the back of his spine and pressing. She tried to massage his back and everywhere she touched felt better. He smiled for a moment, remembering that she was a doctor and how he had never considered that in his interactions with her for real.

He pushed her legs up higher, pulling her ass off the ground, letting her asshole open under him so he could place his dick right at the opening. She pulled him harder into her, moving her hands down to his ass and spreading him open. Jonah let her fuck herself in the ass with his dick, back and forth in the flickering candle light.

He put his hands on her face, caressing her as she clung to him. "You're the best thing I own."

She nodded over and over, holding his eyes in her stare. Jonah felt Eve's hands on his back and she climbed on him, her own strap on pushing and filling him slowly. Giselle spread him open as she lazily fucked him into her. He knew she wanted to say it too, just as he had to Giselle. He believed it was true, even if she never said it.

That he was the best thing she owned.

***

Humans, across the galaxy, are a variable species. And color is a component of that. This is determined by tiny organic compounds in their skin called melanocytes. They respond to Ultraviolet light and adjust the color of skin. There are two specific types. Eumelanin adjusts the brown and black scale of skin, while pheomelanin adjusts the yellow and red scale. A yellow sun alone can trigger these to produce colors from pale brownish-white to dark blue black. When combined with a blue sun, the colors can be fantastically more variable, producing people who are bright yellow, pink, even deep red and maroon. Yleros' twin suns birthed a wide range of colors, nearly across the entire spectrum. They even spawned people who were chalk white with dark blue black hair, evolutionary curiosities triggered when the types of melanocytes cancelled each other out.

The platform containing the portal to Yleros was alive with color. People in familiar colors to Jonah stood next to people in colors that looked like cgi makeup smooth across the entirety of their skin. Red people, Pink people, starkly white ones. People as dark as the bluest black paint. This was a collage of every color the twin suns of Yleros could produce.

Auroketh and Solara

Jonah would read every word that Eve had written, wrapped up in big, thick, beautiful volumes.

He would commit them to memory

They stepped forward on the platform as each group moved through its liquid silvery surface. After each, the women controlling it would check to ensure the fidelity of the transport, talk together, smile.

Laugh.

There was no urgency. The artificial shell of Earth had months to go before impact, when the asteroid would pierce the thin manufactured layer under the pacific ocean, causing the oceans to rush into the empty core of the planet, creating windstorms that would devastate continents and leave an uninhabitable husk behind.

In other parts of the world, platforms like this were delivering people to their choice of worlds, other artificial planets Yleros had created and given their autonomy.

Bako, a strange planet where intimacy was reserved for friends and family, and sex freely distributed amongst people who would never see each other again.

Archon, a violent and regressive world where men are considered superior and in charge, doing what they want to the women around them. A world with strange and visceral beauties of its own, but one that fails time and time again to advance far.

Or Shekaru, a world defined by age, where citizens lose all rights to their bodies once they reach the age of 18 and only gradually reclaim them, becoming autonomous at the age of 40. It's a planet where elderly magnates control harems of 20 year olds, making all decisions for them, trading them like currency.

Madara, a planet operated by stark white people who use the population as food, forcing them to lactate constantly for their pleasure and satisfaction.

Or Dabba, a world starkly split down the middle between human pets and human owners, with no possibility of switching categories, a place of bizarre pleasures and just as intense violations.

Jonah looked around for Oyelo. He was not on the platform. He wasn't sure what his decision was, if he went elsewhere.

He knew Keith had left the day before with Marissa and Grey. He sent him a long message filled with technical jargon Jonah would need to piece through and think about.

They would have time.

Marissa's message was shorter.

See you on the other side, boss.

Despite having been her boss for a grand total of a month, this was the first time she said it. He laughed. This was her way of conjuring up their working relationship, which, now that he had the clarity to review it, was entirely about her doing everything she could for him. Telling him what she could. Showing him what she could.

Being close to him when she could.

He looked forward to seeing her again.

There weren't many people on the platform. Jonah saw one other man, a muscular Latin man with a silk shirt, open widely at the chest. He nodded and received a smile in return.

Only one other man.

Giselle leaned into him with a wide smile on her face. Jonah thought about the pips on her inner thigh. He wished he could kiss them right now. He wished he could show her that they meant everything to him, even though they weren't needed or used.

Eve adjusted his hair as the 4 women in front of them went through the portal.

There was laughter in the room, rising over the electronic hum of the device as it sent people an impossibly long distance away. He considered what Marissa had said about the job of the queen on the chessboard and for the first time in a long time, felt caught up. He wasn't one or two moves ahead or several turns behind.

He was part of the turn.

Where the job of the queen was to protect her king.